D1433573

By the same author
CHARLES WATERTON
THE EMPEROR'S LAST ISLAND
DAISY BATES IN THE DESERT
THE BOOK OF COLOUR

THE LEPER'S COMPANIONS

Julia Blackburn

JONATHAN CAPE

LONDON

Published by Jonathan Cape 1999

2 4 6 8 10 9 7 5 3

Copyright © Julia Blackburn 1999

Julia Blackburn has asserted her right under the Copyright, Designs
and Patents Act 1988 to be identified as the author of this work

This book is sold subject to the condition that it shall not,
by way of trade or otherwise, be lent, resold, hired out, or otherwise
circulated without the publisher's prior consent in any form of binding or
cover other than that in which it is published and without a
similar condition including this condition being imposed
on the subsequent purchaser

First published in Great Britain in 1999 by
Jonathan Cape
Random House, 20 Vauxhall Bridge Road,
London SW1V 2SA

Random House Australia (Pty) Limited
20 Alfred Street, Milsons Point, Sydney,
New South Wales 2061, Australia

Random House New Zealand Limited
18 Poland Road, Glenfield,
Auckland 10, New Zealand

Random House South Africa (Pty) Limited
Endulini, 5A Jubilee Road, Parktown 2193, South Africa

Random House UK Limited Reg. No. 954009

A CIP catalogue record for this book
is available from the British Library

ISBN 0224-05127-X

Papers used by Random House UK Limited are natural,
recyclable products made from wood grown in sustainable forests.
The manufacturing processes conform to the environmental
regulations of the country of origin

Typeset by Deltatype Ltd, Birkenhead

Printed and bound in Great Britain by
Creative Print and Design (Wales), Ebbw Vale

for several people, with love and gratitude

Man, too, hurries,
Eats, couples, buries,
He is an animal also
With a hey ho melancholy,
Away with it, let it go.

Stevie Smith, 'Away Melancholy'

One

O ne day in the month of September when the low
autumn sun was casting long shadows across the
grass, she lost someone she had loved. It does not
matter who that person was or what sort of love it had
been. The fact was that he had gone and she
remained.

She knew it would take at least two years to recover
from the first shock of the loss; to disentangle her
body from his body, her memories from his memories, her life from his life. What she wanted to do now
was to bang the door shut on this present time by
setting out on a journey to some distant country and
to remain there until the present had blurred and
shifted and become indistinguishable from the past.
But that was not possible. She had to stay where she
was. She had to sit still and try to be patient, even
though her mind was trapped like a wild thing in a

cage, zigzagging backwards and forwards, desperate to find a means of escape.

She was terribly afraid. All her old fears had stirred themselves and were lumbering towards her through the tunnels of the past. They crowded around her, the quick and the dead, the forgotten and the remembered. They walked with hard sharp feet across her scalp. They sat there in the shadows, watching her. They were cold and without mercy.

She searched for images that might help her. She saw herself climbing up something like a stem; step by determined step with her fingers clasped so tight that the bones showed white at the knuckles.

She saw herself clinging to a raft. All the land that was ever in the world had disappeared. She could feel the sun on her back, the salt on her lips, the lurching of the waves beneath her body. She raised her head to look up and within the dazzle of light she could just see the thin line of the horizon where the water and the air merged together. That became her destination.

She saw herself as a snake or a spider or any other creature that becomes trapped within the confinement of its own skin and at a certain point needs to split through the outer casing and shuffle it off. She had once watched a snake during the final stage of this transformation. It was lying in the dappled shadow of a tree, as exhausted as a baby that had just been born.

Its new skin was shiny and slippery with life while the old one was white and dry, paper-thin and empty. When she picked it up it rustled softly and she felt she was holding a ghost in her hands.

She could imagine the shell of her own body like that: a shed skin with everything remembered on it from the whirling pattern at the tip of each finger, to the ridge of bones down the back, the curve of the ear, the mouth, the nose. She could see it being lifted up by a gust of wind and carried away and she felt a strange sense of relief when it had gone.

There was a village not far from where she lived. It was close to the sea and when the tide was out the shallow water was pulled back to reveal a huge expanse of rippling sand. The place had such a quality of silence and emptiness to it that sometimes, especially at night, she could find quiet just by imagining herself there. She would walk in her mind across the sand, feeling its ridges under her bare feet, and she would look at the sea and be comforted.

At one end of the village was a very old church; a yew tree stood close to the entrance gate, wild flowers bloomed among the grass, the gravestones were pockmarked by lichen and the weather. A mermaid with sharp teeth and a lascivious smile was carved

3

above the east door and a man with leaves in his hair leered down from a corner of the roof and vomited a stream of water from his open mouth when it was raining.

The air inside the church was damp and cold even on a summer's day and the light had a dim underwater quality to it. A fragment of the original stained glass had survived in one of the windows. It showed an angel with narrow seagull wings sprouting from his back and pointed feathers covering the nakedness of his body. His feet were bare with long toes and he was marooned on a little patch of black-and-white tiled floor with an expanse of plain glass all around him. The expression on his face was gentle and compassionate and sometimes she would sit beside him in her thoughts until their eyes met across the infinite space that divided them and she was comforted.

And then one night in the month of February when the east wind was bitterly cold and she felt so sad she didn't know what to do, she found herself going down the main street of the village. The ground beneath her feet was as hard as rock and deeply rutted by the wheels of carts. The houses on either side of her were small and battered; they reminded her of the nests of birds, as if something like a swallow could have made them from river silt and twigs. The church was newly built, the stones yellow and clean. Everything was

4

different to how she had known it and yet she was shocked by the sense of intense familiarity that surrounded her, the sense of coming home.

Following a path that led to the sea, she reached a rickety wooden hut and a few fishing boats. She accidentally trod on a pile of empty oyster shells and felt them splintering under her feet.

A dog with pale eyes watched as she approached and that surprised her because she had somehow presumed there would be no life here, nothing apart from the shifting of wind and sunlight and the movement of the waves.

She sat with her back to the hut and looked out across the shimmering expanse of sand and sea. 'I have left one place and come to another,' she thought to herself. 'I have stepped out of the time I was in and now I will be here for a while, until things change and pass.'

Two

I was sitting with my back propped against a wooden hut and I was lost in thought, although if anyone had asked me what I was thinking about I would not have had an answer. I was drifting in the dark while all around me the sun was bright and the sky was blue and the air was filled with that yearning cry of seabirds which can so easily bring me close to tears.

Far away on the glistening sand I saw the silhouetted figure of a man bending over something that lay heaped at his feet. It could have been part of a wrecked ship, the trunk of a tree, a bundle of sail. It could have been a fish or a seal or even a person drowned and washed ashore by the tide.

I knew I could pull the whole image nearer to me just by concentrating on it and then I would understand what was happening, but for the moment I chose to leave it undisturbed. Even from this distance

I could sense that the man was fascinated by the thing he had found, but afraid of it as well.

I became aware of someone sitting next to me, his back also leaning against the hut. It was an old man busy mending the broken mesh of a fishing net and singing to himself in a soft monotone as he struggled with the task. His fingers were bunched together like the feet of dead birds and I could feel the tiredness in them and the ache. I knew that in a few days he would be setting out alone in a boat and he would never return to this place, but for now he was here in the sunshine with the sound of his own voice echoing around his head.

I got up and followed the path that led to the village. Mud as hard as stone and grass burnt yellow by the last frost. Nervous chickens scratching for food, a goat tethered to a post, a pig in a pen and a dog with pale eyes watching me. There were people here as well and I could recognize each one of their restless faces although I could not necessarily put a name to them. Even the smiling mermaid carved above the church door and the man with a wide mouth through which the rainwater streamed were as familiar to me as the details of my own life.

The first to move close was a young woman called Sally, the fisherman's daughter. She had gap teeth, rough awkward hands and a round moon face in which the shadows of her own uncertainty were clearly visible. She blushed easily and I could feel how the sudden heat swept across the surface of her skin, making her tremble with confusion.

The shoemaker's wife was next, with big breasts and softly curling hair, her body heavy with the weight of the baby she was carrying: an elbow pushing sharp against the inside of her womb, a head poised above the bone cup of the pelvis, ready for the slow fall. Only a few more days and the process of birth would begin. This was to be her last child.

Her husband the shoemaker was there working at his bench, his shoulders hunched forward. He looked tired and the blindness which would make him feel cut off from the world was already closing in, tightening its grip. The priest was standing silently beside him, staring towards me but not seeing me. I recognized him as the angel from the church window, but then again as someone I had once known long ago.

I walked on through the village. Walls were pulled back like curtains so that I could see inside the houses. In one there was a woman lying in the sour stink of a dark room while a mass of devils crawled over her naked body. Her husband was with her, and even though his face was turned from me, I was suddenly afraid of him.

In another room in another house a woman was sitting upright in bed while all her life walked before her eyes, fast and then slow, the years unfolding into each other as she watched them.

There was the man who was old enough to remember the time when the Great Pestilence had come to the village. And there was the red-haired girl and the man with a red tongue and all the others who lived here; a crowd of them jostling together.

Which was when I saw the leper, or to be more precise I heard him, since it was the beating of the wooden clapper which warned me of his approach. He was just passing the boundary stone close to the last house and was walking straight towards me. His body was draped in a long brown cloak and his face was shielded by a hood.

The leper was the only one here who was a complete stranger to me. I knew nothing about where he had come from or where he was going. I had no idea of what he had looked like before he became ill or how badly he had been disfigured by the sickness. He walked past me without saying a word and he was gone.

I went back along the path that led to the wooden hut and the fishing boats. I had decided to see what it was that the man had found washed up by the tide.

Three

The man was poised in indecision, staring at the thing which lay heaped at his feet. I saw then that it was not a human corpse, or the trunk of a tree, or a bundle of sail that he had found, but a mermaid. She was lying face down, her body twisted into a loose curl, her hair matted with scraps of seaweed.

The year was fourteen hundred and ten and it was very early in the morning with the sun pushing its way gently through a covering of mist that floated aimlessly over the land and the water.

The man had never seen a mermaid before except for the one carved in stone above the east door of the church. She had very pointed teeth and a double tail like two soft and tapering legs, while this one had a single tail which could have belonged to a large halibut or a cod.

The man stepped forward and squatted down beside her. The pattern of her interlinking scales glinted with an oily light. He stroked them along the direction in which they lay and they were wet and slippery, leaving a coating of slime on his palm. But when his hand moved over the pale skin of her back it was dry and cold and as rough as a cat's tongue.

He lifted a hank of dark hair, feeling its weight. Little translucent shrimps were tangled within its mesh and struggling to free themselves. A yellow crab scuttled around the curve of the waist and dropped out of sight.

He hesitated for a moment but then he took hold of the mermaid's shoulders and rolled her over. The sand clung in patches on her body like the map of some forgotten country. Her nipples were as red as sea anemones. Her navel was deep and round. Her eyes were wide open and as blue as the sky could ever be. As he gazed at her a lopsided smile drifted over her face.

He had presumed that she was dead and with the shock of her being alive he let out a cry and jumped to his feet. He turned and began to run as fast as he could over the ridges of muddy sand and towards the village.

I watched as he trampled on the grey scrub of sea lavender and the low samphire bushes, their thin skins so easily broken. But he trod more carefully once he had reached the strip of pale stones littered with the

11

sharp empty shells of clams and oysters, and with his heart thumping in his throat he was beside the fishing boats and the wooden hut battered out of shape by the north wind.

The old fisherman was sitting there just as before, his legs stretched out stiffly in front of him and his bones aching. He made no response when the young man tried to explain what the sea had thrown onto the land; he didn't even raise his head to look at the speaker.

The young man ran on again until he had arrived at the first house of the village. The shoemaker's wife was standing by the door, her arms cradling her huge belly.

'There is a mermaid!' he said to her, but she was lost in thought and hardly heard him, although her baby lurched violently inside her womb as if it was shocked by the news. She remembered that later.

The man went into the house and from a back room he fetched one of those narrow wooden spades that are used for digging lugworms. Then he returned the way he had come. He meant to bury the mermaid even if she was still alive and his task made him walk slowly now, with the solemnity of an executioner.

He looked out across the expanse of sand shimmering like an ocean of calm water. He saw how a flock of gulls had settled in a noisy mass on the place where the mermaid was lying. As he drew closer they lifted, screaming and turning into the air.

But the mermaid had gone. Nothing remained of her except for a single lock of dark hair which resembled a ribbon of torn seaweed.

Nevertheless the man dug a hole as deep as a grave: the salty water seeping into it, the sides crumbling away and seeming to melt like snow. And as he dug the surface brightness of the sand was replaced by greasy layers of black and grey mud smelling of age and decay.

When the hole was ready he picked up the hair and dropped it in, covering it over quickly and stamping it down. He marked the place with a big black stone.

That evening he sat with the old fisherman drinking from a jug of beer and going over and over the story of what he had seen and what he had done. During the night his wife Sally shook him awake because she could hear the sound of a woman crying, desperate and inconsolable. On the following morning a cow died for no good reason and the shoemaker's wife gave birth to a baby with the head of a monstrous fish which only lived for a few hours.

Everyone agreed that this must be the mermaid's fault and they told the priest to do something. So the priest went with the man to where the hair was buried. He took a holy candle with him which kept on going out in the wind and he had a bottle of holy water to sprinkle over the sand. In his spidery handwriting he had copied three paternosters onto a scrap of vellum and he tucked these under the black stone while reciting a prayer to protect them all from harm.

After that things were quiet again for a while, but it was as if a lid had been clamped down on a pot that was bound to boil over sooner or later. The mermaid had disturbed the pattern of life in the village and people waited with growing apprehension for what might follow.

The man who had stroked her rough skin had a dream in which she slithered over his body like a huge eel and wrapped her tail tight around his legs. He was crying when he woke up.

He kept on stumbling against her image in a corner of his mind. Whenever he went out with his boat he would hope to find her glistening among the fish he had caught in his nets. He began to travel further and further from the shore, searching for her.

Four

The old fisherman stopped mending his nets. His hands were stiff and painful and he laid them side by side on his lap, the fingers bunched together like the feet of dead birds.

For as long as he kept singing he was cocooned in images: he was out at sea among the rolling waves of a storm, the backs of whales and silver fishes breaking through the surface of the water all around him. A catch of living things was thrashing at his feet in the boat, struggling for breath. But then as soon as his voice was silent, he was only here, frail in the sunshine and thinking about his daughter Sally.

She was not yet fifteen but already pregnant with her first child. The old fisherman was afraid that the birth might kill her and with that thought he realized he could not bear to lose her. She was what connected him to the village and to the land itself and if she was gone he would be homeless.

Every night he dreamt of his fear. He saw her as a child giving birth to a child much bigger than she was. He saw her body split open like a ripe seedpod and a mass of maggot babies crawling over her, eating her flesh until there was nothing left but the clean white bones. He told no one of these dreams because that would only make them more solid and more dangerous.

Sometimes in the morning he would wake to find her beside his bed, a tiny moon-faced child who had just learnt to walk, staring at him with all the tenderness and seriousness of the very young.

He rarely went to sea these days, but when he did, Sally was the one who waited for his return. She would stand on the beach pulling at the thread which connected them as if he was a fish on a line.

Her husband was also uneasy about what was happening to her; the skin of her swollen belly luminous and blue so that you could see every detail of the vast creature inhabiting her.

He gave her oily herrings to eat, saying the oil would help the baby slip out. He lay awake at night, watching her in the moonlight, her face flickering with shifting emotions, now peaceful, now in despair.

The straw of the mattress rustled as she moved and turned and she often talked in her sleep, although he could never understand what she was saying. He stroked her damp skin and as he did so she sometimes became the mermaid lying next to him, rough and cold and smiling, with hair that wrapped itself around his fingers.

On the morning when the waters broke and soaked into the straw they fetched the woman who knew how to deliver babies. She brought a flask of water that had been used to wash the hands of a murderer, ground pepper to help with the contractions and a greasy salve smelling of rancid butter to rub over the tight belly.

The yellow sunlight flickered on the walls of the room and the bed creaked when the girl was thrown sideways with the first spasm of pain.

'You have to let go,' the midwife said. 'It will be easier once you have let go.'

She unplaited Sally's flat hair and spread it loose across her shoulders. She opened the lid of a wooden chest and took out the few clothes and the sheepskin rug it contained, scattering them over the floor. She opened the door of a cupboard and removed a bundle of knotted ropes that had been left there, carefully undoing the knots and laying the pieces in straight lines. The spasms continued and became more violent than ever.

Sally's husband was sitting in the room next door, close to the smoking fire, gutting herrings and rubbing them with salt. When he heard his wife screaming he sharpened his blade and continued with his work.

Her father was down by the shore but he heard the screams as well. They echoed in his head like the cries of seabirds.

He rose slowly to his feet and walked to the church. Pushing the door open, he went to stand in front of the painting of Margaret of Antioch, the saint who is able to help women in labour.

The painting was done on wood in dark rich colours. It was divided into six squares and each square showed a stage of the saint's life. In the first square Margaret was cast out of her house by her cruel father and you could see her walking into the hills with her head bowed. In the second square the Roman Patriarch, whose name the fisherman could not remember, tried to rape her, but she resisted him. In the third square she was hung on a rack that was similar to the racks used in the village for drying fish. Two soldiers were scraping at her body with an iron hook so that the bones were revealed and the blood fell from her like red water. Next she was put into prison and the bars of her cage were all around her.

While she was in prison the Devil appeared in the form of a green dragon and with its hot breath it sucked the saint into its mouth. You could see her standing with bare feet on the soft red tongue, the row of teeth hanging down above her like icicles around the eaves of a house. But now that she was inside the body of the dragon she held up an iron cross and spoke the name of God. The dragon exploded and she was delivered safely back into the world and out of danger.

The old fisherman stood there in the dim light of the church, gazing at the white face of the saint, at her gold halo like the sun at harvest time, at the dragon's scaly skin, the teeth, the blood. And he began to sing the story of what was happening. He sang the saint out of the sorrow of leaving home, out of the fear of rape. He gave her courage when the metal hook bit into her flesh. He comforted her in the loneliness of the prison and he prayed for her when she was trapped inside the dragon's body until he could feel her breaking through and escaping.

When the story was completed he told the saint that if his daughter survived he would show his thanks by setting out as a pilgrim to Jerusalem. He would go in a boat across the North Sea and then he would walk to Venice where a ship could take him to the port of Jaffa. From there he knew it was not far to the Holy City. If he died on the way he would accept that the saint was exchanging his life for his daughter's.

He returned to the house and went to sit by the fire next to his son-in-law. The noise had subsided and everything was poised in quiet anticipation. The midwife appeared with blood on her clothes and said the two men could enter the bedroom. There they found Sally as limp as a fish with a little baby suckling at her breast.

Her father fulfilled the vow he had made to Saint Margaret. He left early one morning and his boat faded from sight as it approached the horizon.

Before he went he explained to Sally what it was that he had to do. She did not disagree with him or try to make him stay but as soon as he had gone she was as desolate as a child for whom the present moment has no end.

Her husband spent more and more time out at sea searching for the mermaid, coming back with his nets empty. Finally he did not come back at all for several days. Sally found him washed up by the tide, naked and cold, not far from the black stone under which the lock of hair was buried.

Five

A group of people from the village were running to the house of the woman who saw devils. Sally was there with them and so was the shoemaker and his wife, the red-haired girl, the man who could remember the Great Pestilence and several others whose faces were turned from me.

They came to a halt in front of an open door, jostling awkwardly against each other like sheep in a pen.

'We must do something!' said one voice and everyone waited to be told what was to be done.

'She has bitten her husband who is such a gentle man!' said another voice, urgent with indignation. 'She has tried to murder her new baby! She is tearing at her own flesh and pulling out her hair! She can see thousands of devils, the room is thick with them!'

Even though there no wind, the door was swinging backwards and forwards on its hinges and the creaking sound it made was like a warning. Only a few of the people gathered outside were brave enough to cross the threshold into the kitchen with its smell of woodsmoke and through into the bedroom where the air was sour and oppressive.

A piece of leather had been hung across the window. It flapped like the wings of Satan himself, sitting there hunched and terrible, watching what was going on.

The shoemaker's wife stepped forward and unhooked the leather from the nails holding it in place. At once a stream of pale light spread out over the walls and ceiling and over the rushes on the floor.

The woman's two youngest children were huddled silent in a corner of the room with their arms wrapped tightly around each other and their eyes wide. Her husband was beside the door, four red scratches running down his cheek and a thin trickle of blood dripping from his ear where he had been bitten. The baby was in a cradle and appeared to be asleep.

The woman was lying on the big four-poster bed, but the moment the covering was removed from the window she hid herself under the blanket so that she was reduced to nothing more than the heaving of the breath in her body. You could hear her breathing too, a rasping, hissing sound like the blacksmith's bellows.

Everyone stared at the bed with its mound of

hidden life. It was a very old bed that had been in the family for generations. The four carved oak posts were polished by the many hands that had grasped them. A jumble of names, dates and initials had been carved into the slab of wood that was the headboard and you could also distinguish the shape of a heart pierced by an arrow and a curious prancing creature with a spike growing out of its head that must have represented a unicorn. The woman's mother had kept a record of the arrival of her numerous babies with a little line for each one and the line crossed out with a slash of the knife if that baby died. Her daughter had considered marking the birth of her babies in the same way but she couldn't bear the idea of crossing through the lines. Instead she had simply carved her own intial, M for Mary, and next to it another M for her husband Michael.

She remained quite still under the scratching weight of the blanket that covered her. Her naked body felt huge and hollow. Her breasts tingled with the milk she was carrying and she could smell the cloying sweetness leaking from her swollen nipples. She remembered again how sad and lonely she had suddenly felt when this last baby slipped out of her womb and into the world.

It must be like that when you die, she thought, and the soul has to take its leave of the body. For three days it hovers close and then it must go and never return. That is when your body begins to change and turns into nothing more than a corpse needing to be buried under the ground. That was when the devils had come to her, three days after the baby's birth, while she was feeling like an empty and abandoned shell.

It was her husband Michael who had seen the devils first. He told her how they were crawling all over her, their mouths filled with flames, their teeth stained with blood, their goat penises as sharp as spears. She could hear him explaining what he had seen to the people who were gathered in the room now. His voice was clear and authoritative and she could imagine the horror on everyone's face.

From within the hot darkness she began to tremble and cry out as if in pain.

'Look, she is fighting with the devils!' said Michael, and then he began to shout, 'We must save her! We must tie her down!'

She wanted to escape but it was not possible. Someone grabbed her by the shoulders and it felt as if someone else was sitting on her head. Her hands were extracted from under the blanket and tied together at the wrist before being attached by another cord to the bedpost. Her feet were exposed and were also bound and tied. Only then were they ready to pull back the covering from her face.

They were all staring at her. 'You are safe now,' said Michael in his gentle voice and he stroked her hair with his fingers. With all her strength she twisted round and tried to bite him, her teeth lightly grazing his skin. He smiled as he withdrew his hand but when she looked at him all that she could see was his savagery and his cruelty. She realized then that she was more afraid of him than any number of devils.

It was decided that someone must stay with her to keep watch, and the shoemaker's wife said she would be glad to. They gave her a big chair to sit in and she pulled it close to the bed.

Once the others had gone and the room was quiet the shoemaker's wife made Mary more comfortable, loosening the ropes that were too tight on her wrists and putting a feather bolster behind her back. Then she began to talk.

She told Mary what when she gave birth to a baby with the head of a monstrous fish people had said that this was the Devil as well and they blamed it on the mermaid. 'But I loved him all the same,' she said, 'and so did my husband. He died on the day he was born and we had to bury him outside the churchyard, so now we don't know where he is.'

Mary smiled. She was watching particles of dust

floating in the beam of sunlight that came in through the window. Each one was a gleaming speck of powdered gold. 'They look like angels,' she thought to herself. 'An army of bright angels has come to drive away the devils.'

Six

The shoemaker and his wife were sitting side by side in another room in this village that has become a sanctuary for my restless thoughts.

He was quite a small man. His eyes and his hair were grey. The skin of his face was as pale as parchment and stretched so tight across the bones of his skull that only when you looked carefully could you see the tracery of thin lines showing his age.

His wife was the same height and with a strong body, although her hands and feet were surprisingly delicate. She had pendulous breasts and a softness of skin and hair that had increased over the years. Her eyes were the same colour as her husband's, but with a dark rim around the iris and the pupils were as sensitive as a cat's, expanding and contracting at the slightest change of light.

The physical closeness between these two was apparent in everything they did: the slightest look, the touch of a hand, it was all part of a ritual which reminded them of the sexual act. They had been married for a long time and yet they both often remembered the first night they spent in each other's arms and how their bodies had joined with such ease, the pleasure rising and overflowing and leaving them content.

They had made love in open fields and under the shelter of trees, in darkness and daylight, in winter and summer. They had made love in spite of the fact that a new baby was on the edge of being born or that her menstrual blood was mixing with his seed. The slow process of growing old had hardly diminished the intensity of their desire.

But then everything changed. The shoemaker began to go blind. He noticed it first when he was standing in the church in front of the row of brightly painted alabaster figures crowded along one wall. He realized with a shock that he was unable to tell if that was a dragon crushed under the heel of Saint Michael or a gold key gripped in the hand of Saint Peter. He turned to gaze at the stained-glass window, but all he could see was a shifting pattern of colour in which there was no form: no angels or devils, no Heaven or Hell. It must be the dim light, he told himself, anyone could be confused by it.

Soon the darkness was growing thicker so that he

dreaded opening his eyes in the morning for fear of what else he would not be able to see. And when his wife gave birth to the baby with the head of a monstrous fish he took the creature in his arms but was spared the shock of its deformity and only guessed that it was dead because it was cold. They buried it outside the boundary of the churchyard and as he struggled to see the shape of a wooden box being lowered into the unforgiving earth he knew that something must be done.

'Look at my eyes!' he said to his wife as they made their way back along the village street. 'Look at them! What is wrong with them?'

She stopped and pulled his head towards her with firm hands. She put her face close to his so that her warm breath flowed over his skin. She said, 'It's as if milk has been spilt into them. Your eyes are covered with a layer of curdled milk.'

He had no wish to go to a doctor who would only suggest cutting and bleeding, so he went instead to the woman who could use charms and herbs.

She made a mixture out of wild honey and fox fat and the marrow from a roe deer. She sang over it in the name of the Father, the Son and the Holy Ghost as she rubbed it sticky onto his closed eyelids. But it did no good.

He went to the priest. The priest listened quietly

and said the best thing to do was to buy an eye made from wax and take it to the church, leaving it in front of the statue of Saint Clare who could always be trusted to help with such afflictions.

So the shoemaker bought himself two eyes; smooth unblinking things as big as hens' eggs. He kissed them carefully and presented them to the saint.

But his sight only got worse. There was a dark crack opening across the left eye now so that he saw a remnant of the world torn through the middle as if it had been slashed with a sharp knife. A shadow was creeping around the edge of his vision as well, like the sky before the eruption of a thunderstorm.

He became afraid. The fact of seeing so little made him feel as if he no longer existed. He could not bear to touch his wife or to be touched by her because that only hammered more loudly on the door of his isolation. He felt he was being punished for some terrible crime, although he could not think what that crime might be unless it was simply the hugeness of his own despair.

Someone told his wife about a new shrine dedicated to Saint Anselm, with one of the saint's thigh bones encased in a golden casket. She decided to take her husband there.

It was a journey of many hours to reach the shrine and when they arrived the shoemaker sat exhausted with his head in his hands. He had no expectation of recovery and felt that he must learn to accept the damnation of darkness that had come upon him.

But his wife was filled with a rush of wild energy. She stood facing the shrine and began to shout at it in a loud voice, 'Give him back his sight! Give my husband back his sight!'

She wasn't praying to the saint or begging for help, she was demanding what she felt to be hers by right. She shouted for six days and six nights. At first her voice was clear and strident, but gradually it weakened until it was nothing more than a grating whisper, although the indignation within it was never diminished. She didn't pause to eat or sleep, she didn't even defecate. She just stood rooted to the earth and shouted, her words like waves beating against a rock.

A crowd of people had gathered around the shrine to find out what was happening and there was a sense of growing excitement in the air.

And then the miracle happened. The scales that had covered the shoemaker's eyes fell away. He saw the blue of the sky, the green of the grass, the intricate dazzling beauty of leaves and trees. But he also saw the mass of staring faces gathered around him.

All the people who had witnessed the miracle wanted to have a share of the blessing. They reached forward to touch the shoemaker, to cut off a piece of his cloak or a lock of his hair. They clung around him, asking questions and demanding his attention. He was horrified by their ugliness and their cruelty. Overwhelmed by panic, he ran stumbling into the safety of the forest.

His wife found him there a few hours later. He was lying face down under the shelter of some low branches with only his feet visible.

She heaved him up into a sitting position. She tried to kiss him and comfort him but he struggled to be free of her as well. 'Leave me alone, I want to be dead,' he said and he began to cry.

They made their way home slowly and she had to steer his steps as if he was still blind. When they reached their house in the village he rushed into a room at the back and refused to come out. He cried continuously and would not be comforted.

'He has gone mad,' his wife said. 'First he was blind and now he is mad.'

She waited for several weeks in the hope that the madness would lift, but when nothing had changed she returned on her own to the shrine.

She stood in front of the saint. She asked him what he thought he was doing, curing a man like that only to inflict a new pain on him. She shook her fist at the casket. She spat on it. Driven by her own desperation she prised it open, took out the thigh bone and threw it with all her strength into a nearby stream. Then she went home.

Sometimes she sat beside her husband and tried to talk to him about the life they had shared together and how happy they had been, but more often than not she left him there alone with his own thoughts.

Seven

The shoemaker is sitting in the almost dark of his room. 'Everything is because of something,' he says to himself. 'I could see. I was blind. I can see again. Everything is because of something.'

He has grown accustomed to his own tears. He even cries when he is sleeping, the salt water flowing down the sides of his face and collecting in pools in his ears. He doesn't know why he is crying and he has no idea how he could ever stop himself from crying. It has become an aspect of staying alive, like breathing.

He can see a thin strip of light shining around the edge of the closed door. 'It's as if I have been shut out of Heaven,' he says to himself, but when he tries to imagine pulling the door open and stepping through to the other side he cannot do it. 'I am shut in and I am shut out!' he says, speaking aloud now and startled by the sound of his own voice.

His mouth is dry. He runs his tongue sticky and

slow around the edge of his lips and that makes a noise too, a crackling sound like the flames of a little fire.

He leans back against the wall and listens to the movements of the house. There is a rustling in the roof which is either rats or pigeons, the creaking of a floorboard from the weight of someone walking on it and a soft thumping sound which he cannot identify. It might be his wife in the kitchen making bread. Or it might be that she is making love with another man and what he hears is the beating of flesh on flesh.

A child is laughing. It is probably one of his own children but he cannot guess which one. Their identities have become blurred. They are strangers who laugh and cry in other rooms and who sometimes come and hover at his side, hoping for a sign or a kind word.

Everything is because of something. The church bell starts to count the hours but he misses the first echoing reverberation of metal against metal and so he has no idea of the time. A dog barks a warning and then yelps as if someone has kicked it into silence. A calf is led past the front of the house, bellowing with despair.

He often wonders if animals could learn to talk. He once had a dog which seemed to be about to say something; it would stare at him with its mouth open and the words just out of reach. And the old woman who made the ointment for his eyes kept a pig which could say 'Goodbye, God bless you,' but it died before he was born. His mother had heard it.

His mother was haunted by her memory of the Great Pestilence. When he was a child she would sometimes cry out because she could see a pile of corpses heaped up in the corner of the room in which they were standing. Then he would hold her legs as tight as he could until her terror had passed and the room was empty again. He remembers the smell of her as he buried his face against her skirts: as salt and sweet as a fish. Later he discovered that other women smelt the same. Different, but always the same.

Everything is because of something and now that a silence has returned he becomes aware of the noises inside his own head. There is a distant roar like the wind among the trees, but there is also a plaintive high-pitched whistling sound, as if a solitary bird was singing within its cage of bone.

The shoemaker lies very still on his back. He takes a breath of air and pulls it up through the soles of his feet, along the rippling length of his spine and out at the top of his head. Then he pulls the breath down again, from head to foot. He can see the air like a silver thread running through the length of his body. He is stitching himself together with silver threads.

He places a little fish within the hollow cavity of his skull. It is a single glittering fish; no, it is a shoal of fishes and each one is no bigger than his thumb. He drops them skittering with life into a clear stream that is so cold it makes his bones ache when he holds his hand in it. The water is racing over pebbles that are speckled like plovers' eggs. The fish are moving in perfect unison; when one turns they all turn, when one holds itself steady they all hold themselves steady. The shoemaker watches them for a long time.

He hears footsteps on the stairs, a hesitation, the lifting of the latch and the door swings open. Instinctively he closes his eyes against the intrusion of the daylight.

'Who is there?' he asks, his voice querulous through the tears.

He can feel the presence of someone drawing closer and squatting down beside him. He can smell his wife. He suddenly remembers the slippery softness of her belly and her thighs.

She traces the outline of his face with the tips of her fingers. She leans forward so that her breath flows over him like warm water. Her hair trails across his lips. Slowly and methodically she begins to lick the tears away, her tongue running across the closed seam of his eyes.

She clambers on top of him, heavy, salt and sweet,

and she rides him just as she used to do in the past. He had forgotten the intense familiarity of her body. Now that he is caught up in it again the sadness leaves him and he realizes that he has stopped crying.

Eight

The sea along this part of the coast always looks very quiet. Even when the moon is full and the tide at its greatest strength with a storm blowing in from the east, it appears strangely calm and untroubled.

But it is quick. I have watched it rushing over the expanse of mud and pale sand as fast as it takes for you to turn your back, and when you look round again you might find that you are cut off, with the safety of the real shoreline at a far distance. Then it can be very difficult to retrace your steps because in between the shallow lapping waters there are deep channels formed by the meanderings of the river and if you slip into one of them the mud is so oily-soft that you can never be sure of getting a foothold and clambering out again.

I was standing where the river joins the sea, a little way around the curve of the coastline but still in view of the village. The tide was coming in and as it did so it disturbed the many birds that were busy feeding. It was a storm of birds, something I could imagine from a dream but which I have never seen in my waking life. White clouds of avocets and oyster catchers spun before my eyes. Tern and dunlin flew and settled and flew again like gusts of autumn leaves. The air was filled with the noisy complaint of ducks and geese and swans, the creaking of wings, sudden screams and cries.

The sheet of water pulling in towards me and spreading over the sand was as calm as a lake without even a ripple of waves. Rising out of it I could see a smooth mound of land which was turned into an island with every high tide. Its surface was covered with a scattering of coarse grass and a few seals were basking there, knowing what they could easily roll back into the safety of the open sea if there was any sudden danger. The people of the village always referred to it as Catherine's Island because this was where the woman called Catherine came to live, once she had decided to leave her home.

I have often seen Catherine. She has heavy-lidded eyes and when she walks it is with the jerky mechanical movements of a wading bird. She is more solitary and remote than anyone I have ever known.

Catherine was married once, but her husband vanished years ago and she never mentioned him after he had gone. She had no children of her own but she was fond of children in the way that someone else might be fond of stray cats. A huddled group of them would often come to her door, hoping to be invited in to eat honey cakes. Her house was the largest in the village, set slightly apart from the others and constructed around a framework of strong wooden beams.

This house was filled with treasures. There was a painted wooden chest on which two knights on horseback charged towards each other with their lances aimed for the heart while a lady dressed in green waited patiently for the outcome of their fight. There was a rug from the Holy Land, woven in intricate patterns of blue and crimson, and a china pot with a blue dragon crawling around it, his whiskers twirling.

But it was the tapestry that the children loved most. It showed a forest of slender trees surrounding a pretty stone tower. Birds were nesting in the trees and rabbits skittering among the flowers in the grass, but there were no people. It seemed as if they must have been there once, a whole crowd of them talking and laughing together, but then for some reason they had vanished and now all that was left was their absence reverberating among the trees like an echo.

An area about the size of a chessboard in the centre of the tapestry had been cut out and replaced with a piece taken from a different tapestry, presumably because the original had been damaged. The repair was done so well and the colours were so closely matched that you hardly noticed it at first, but when you looked again you saw that instead of the trunks of trees there was a little group of human figures huddled together with their mouths wide open, as if they were surprised by something or were singing together in one voice. There was no way of knowing how many others were there with them or what else was happening in their world.

The children would sit on the floor eating cake and staring at the tapestry, their gaze returning repeatedly to the patch within it that seemed to contain another layer of existence. Later when they walked through the forest or along the coastal path they imagined cutting a hole into the quiet landscape that surrounded them to reveal a fragment of what lay hidden beneath it. Or they would frighten each other by saying they could hear voices singing within the stillness of the day.

One morning when a group of them were in the house, Catherine suddenly let out a little cry and fell to the ground as if she had been shot. She lay on the rug from the Holy Land, her eyes closed and all the colour gone from her cheeks. The children ran out into the road calling for help.

People came quickly from the fields, from the boats by the sea, from their houses. They gathered around the prostrate body and wondered whether Catherine was dead or alive.

When the priest arrived he said there were three signs by which death could be recognized: paleness, coldness and stiffness. He felt the woman's skin and it was cold. He looked at her and she was pale, but when he raised one of her arms it was not stiff. The priest told the others to lift her up carefully and place her on the bed.

She lay there very quiet. Her breathing was so faint it could hardly be detected when a feather was held in front of her lips. Her body was so still it seemed to merge with the thin blankets that covered it. Her face was empty and calm; she looked like the figure of a saint carved in stone.

The priest was convinced she was about to die at any moment and so he came with the oil of Extreme Unction and recited the final prayers for the dead over her. Although she managed to swallow a fragment of the wafer and a sip of the wine, she made no response.

People began to make preparations for the funeral. A shroud was placed neatly folded on the floor beside the bed and the length of the body was measured with a piece of string so that the carpenter could make a coffin. The more curious of the onlookers took this opportunity to explore the house and examine the treasures it contained.

But after three days of flickering on the edge, Catherine slept peacefully and when she woke she was fully recovered. The priest was very shocked by the mistake he had made. He explained to her that she was now, as it were, dead to the world because of the prayers that he had said over her. She must never again wear shoes or eat meat or be intimate with a man. She laughed when he told her this and didn't seem at all upset.

The priest was eager to know if she had any experience of dying that she could share with him, since people were always asking him what they might expect.

She could not remember much, but said she had seen a huge army of men and women walking across the world. 'I think they were on their way to the Holy Land,' she said. 'They swept past me, wave upon wave of them, as if they were everyone who had ever lived and died since the beginning of time and I was able to join them. It was a vision.'

Soon afterwards Catherine gathered up all her possessions and distributed them among the people of the village. One of the children received the tapestry. The shoemaker's wife got the pot with the dragon on it and the woman who saw devils suddenly had a rug to place over the rushes on her bedroom floor.

Catherine had quite a lot of money in a leather purse and she took it to the priest. She asked him to use it to go on a pilgrimage to Jerusalem. He could take two or three others from the village. There was no hurry. When he got there she wanted him to say a prayer for her in the Church of the Holy Sepulchre and to bring back a flask of water from the River Jordan. 'I think that is what is expected of me,' she said, in a matter-of-fact voice.

She arranged to have a little house built on the mound of land they called The Island. It was just a circular hut made of mud and wood with an open fire on the earth floor and a box bed filled with straw.

From that time on people referred to her as The Dead Woman. They gave her food and firewood and clothing when she needed it because they were sure it would bring them luck when it was their turn to die, but they never spoke to her and she never asked them to.

Quite often when the tide was out she could be seen threading her way with awkward halting steps towards the village, following the slippery paths on bare feet, a storm of birds flying around her head where she had disturbed them. And when the tide was racing in she would be there in front of her hut, watching the water spreading across the land and separating her from the shore.

Nine

I entered a room in a house in the village and there was an old lady sitting very upright in her bed. She wasn't ill or in pain and she wasn't even particularly tired. She had decided to stay in bed because she needed to think about her life.

She said everything had happened much too fast, the years racing ahead of her while she ran after them, calling for them to wait. Now she was going to sit still and let the past walk before her eyes like dancers on a stage, obedient to her command.

She had made the decision early one morning, waking out of a vague dream and urgent with the need to begin. Her granddaughter the red-haired girl was sleeping in the bed beside her and she shook her roughly awake.

'I need to get ready,' she said, as if that was explanation enough. 'Fetch me the white shift from the chest, the one with the lace around the sleeves and neck. I wore it on the night of my marriage and I haven't worn it since. Get it now and hurry!'

The red-haired girl lived alone with her grandmother and she was accustomed to doing what she was told. She went obediently to the chest on bare feet, and struggled with the weight of the lid.

'Be quick!' said the old woman, rising into a sitting position with her naked flesh heaped on itself in soft folds and creases. 'Dress me!' and she held her arms above her head while the girl stood beside her and pulled on the shift, careful not to damage the fragile cloth.

'How do I look?' said the old woman.

'You look lovely,' said the girl, stroking the mottled patterns of damp and mould on the white linen, feeling the intricacy of lace between her fingers.

'You must do my hair,' said the old woman. 'And you can see if I have many lice. I felt them moving about all last night, muddling my thoughts. Perhaps there are more of them now that the weather has turned warm.'

The girl fetched a comb and a bowl of water. She climbed onto the bed and squatting beside her grandmother she began combing and parting, combing and parting, disentangling the pale sleepy bodies from their nesting places and setting them to sail like little boats in the water, their legs waving feebly.

47

'You can catch them with a piece of bread spread with bird lime,' said the old woman. 'You leave it out on the pillow at night. And a rag dipped in honey is good for flies, but the honey drips. How many have we got?'

'Ten,' said the girl, counting the floating bodies to the highest number she knew.

'So are we ready then?' said the old woman, her grey hair spreading like steam around her tired face and across her shoulders.

'Yes,' said the girl, absent-mindedly holding one of her grandmother's hands in her own, examining the thin skin stretched over the pulsing blue veins.

'Where do you want to begin?' she asked, turning the limp hand over and looking at the mass of lines on the palm.

'As a young girl,' said the old woman rather smugly, 'with your red hair and your face, only it was mine then.'

'Were you young for a long time?' asked the girl.

'Yes,' said her grandmother, 'for a very long time.' And as she spoke the solemn procession of her childhood walked through the room. There were people she knew and people who were strangers but whose faces had lodged themselves in her mind. There were also animals, birds and even fish which had impressed her in some way or another. Noises and smells drifted through her head while the darkness of the night and the brightness of the day repeated itself over and over again as the years moved from one into the next.

She watched them all marching past her bed and when something in particular caught hold of her attention she made it pause so that she could look at it more closely.

There was a painting of Saint Christopher on the end wall of the church in the village where she had lived when she was a child. She gazed now with infinite leisure at the tight curls on his head, the waves and fishes swirling around his big pink legs, the Christ child clinging so tenaciously to his neck. She could feel the movement of his body as he strode forward, the sunlight on his hair, the warmth of his skin, the booming resonance of his voice that could chase away every fear.

When Saint Christopher had gone the acrobats arrived. They announced themselves with the sound of drums and tambourines and tin whistles. There was a girl no older than herself with gold rings in her ears who could walk like a spider across a tightrope while her lizard body could turn and bend and wriggle as if it had no bones to hold it in place. The old woman had always longed to wear those glittering gold rings, to move with that same slippery grace.

The red-haired girl sat patiently beside her grandmother and watched her as she watched, although she could not see what she was seeing.

By mistake the old woman allowed herself to pause in front of the image of a horse in the rain. She felt a sense of dread welling up inside her but she could not remember what was going to happen next. Then once more she felt the shock of terror when the horse toppled over and collapsed into the mud, staring at her with empty dead eyes. She gripped tightly at her granddaughter's hand until the beast had been dragged away and was gone.

Suddenly she saw her father, so thin and frail, sitting by the fire, the red light from the flames dancing on his skin. Her mother was there with him, peeling potatoes, but they ignored each other. 'My mother was a big woman like me,' she said and her granddaughter nodded in agreement because she had been told this before.

It was then that the Bad Winter began. She turned her head away but she could not escape from the ice-bound soil or from the hungry people drifting across the landscape, searching for anything that might serve as food. The houses that had been filled with life were now empty and their windows and open doors stared at her in their desolation.

'That was when I left my village,' she said. 'I was

the only one who did not die. A man who was like Saint Christopher found me. He lifted me onto his back and brought me here. I was afraid of the cries of the seagulls until I got used to them. I had never seen the sea before.'

'I am sometimes afraid of the seagulls,' said the red-haired girl. 'They can be very fierce. I think they pulled the mermaid to pieces and only left a scrap of her hair, but Sally says she escaped and came back later.'

'So then I was here,' said the old woman emphatically, not interested in other people's stories.

The procession was different now. There were fewer strangers, fewer animals, no birds or fish. The distinction between day and night was less clearly defined. People from the past came lumbering noisily into the room and sat themselves down at the end of the bed demanding attention. The red-haired girl still could not see them or hear what they said but she watched her grandmother's response to each new arrival.

The old woman's husband came in and she shouted out his name and ducked her head to avoid a blow from his fist. But then he had gone. 'He's dead now,' she said, with relief and an edge of surprise in her voice.

'Oh good,' said the girl, who had never met him but knew all about his foul temper.

The past was drawing closer and closer to the present now and the old woman's face was becoming luminous and transparent from the effort of remembrance.

'I am getting there,' she said softly, and her granddaughter was startled because the familiar voice had never before sounded so gentle and submissive.

'I am an old woman in bed,' she said at last, grinning rather foolishly as if she had done something wrong and hoped to escape punishment.

She never spoke again. In the morning the red-haired girl woke to find that the body lying beside her was cold and still.

She got dressed and moved around the room, arranging things and putting them in their place before going to fetch the priest. She found a little horn button on the floor and picked it up and dropped it into her pocket. Later she sewed it onto one of her own dresses that had a button missing. It was another way of remembering.

Ten

The leper arrived here in the month of February. The sky on that day was without colour and so empty you could not believe it contained the sun, the moon and all the stars hidden somewhere within its blank immensity. The air was sharp, cutting through closed doors and bolted windows, rasping at naked skin.

It had been a long winter and it was not yet over. Everyone was tired and hungry but they still had to wait for the warmth of the sun to soften the earth and make things grow.

A few cabbages and tufts of curly kale stood lopsided in the fields, their outer leaves burnt by the frost. There were no more potatoes. The carrots had turned to slime in the heap of sand that was supposed to protect them. The remaining scraps of salt bacon tasted as sour as stale beer and the fish were impossible to catch, as if they were clinging to the floor of the ocean in order to keep out of reach of the nets.

It was the first week of Lent and I heard several people joking together in a half-hearted way, saying they would have to stop eating so much rich food and go on a fast in order to remember their sins. I had not seen hunger before, it looked very similar to sadness, I thought.

The leper had made himself a clapper out of two wooden boards bound at one side with a strip of leather. The boards had been the protective cover for a traveller's guidebook to the Holy Land. He had taken the book with him when he went there as a young man long ago and in the years that followed his return he had only to hold it in his hands and he was back with the musty smells of that country, the whirring of cicadas, the relentless heat of the sun.

It had been very strange to unpick the stitches holding the boards in place and put them to this new use. The pages were still bound together and he had wrapped them in a cloth. He had them now in his sack along with a few other possessions.

I watched him walk along the road. On his left he could look out across the grey sea with no sign of a fishing boat, no waves, no birds, nothing for the eye to settle on. On his right there was a brief cluster of birch trees, an empty meadow and then the cultivated field in which the cabbages and the curly kale were growing.

The first of the houses in the village was the one that belonged to Catherine, but now that she had gone from it, it had almost ceased to exist, standing there as insubstantial as a shadow.

The other houses were crammed closely together like swallows' nests under the eaves of a roof. You could just see the yellow stonework of the church over at the far end of the village.

The leper passed a steep bank of grass that would be covered with flowers when spring came, but there were no colours as yet, only the uniformity of an exhausted green.

Just then I saw Sally stepping out of a door and standing in the road with her back turned to me. She was talking to the baby in her arms and her voice carried easily across the stillness of the morning.

'I'll eat primroses for you,' she said. 'I'll eat a whole dish of primroses as soon as they have come. That will thicken my milk and fatten you up.'

The baby began to cry and she hugged it with a sudden fierceness that made it cry even more.

The sound of the clapper was growing stronger now, tentative and yet insistent.

Clack, clack, clack, and Sally turned towards the approaching figure.

Clack, clack, clack, and he was muffled in a long cloak with a hood that concealed his face.

Clack, clack, clack, and it was like the warning cry of a bird when the cat is out hunting.

Clack, clack, clack, and with a shock she realized that a leper was entering the village.

She watched him drawing closer. The baby knocked its head against her breast, making the milk rush and tingle.

'Perhaps he has no hair,' she thought to herself. 'Perhaps he has a hand missing or holes in his body where the flesh has fallen away. He mustn't touch my baby or he might kill it. He mustn't speak to me except with the wind blowing against him. He mustn't look at me because the sickness can jump out from a person's eyes and catch hold of you.'

The leper was close now, but he didn't stop or even slow down. As he passed he said, 'I am going to sit by the wall of the churchyard. Ask the priest to find me there.'

His voice was soft and clear but the accent was very strange and Sally had to run his words several times through her mind before she understood what he was saying. The fact that he came from somewhere far away made her suddenly ashamed of how little she knew of anything beyond the village where she lived.

She went at once to the priest, rushing in on him

where he sat at his desk, copying a prayer onto a piece of vellum.

'There is a leper,' she said, aware of her own awkwardness, her hands chapped by the cold, the weight of the baby pulling at her.

'He has a clapper and he clacks as he walks. That was why I went out. To see what it was. He spoke to me. You must go to him. I'll take you.'

The priest had kept his head bent forward as she spoke and only now did he raise it to look at her. He placed the goose quill and the sharpening knife side by side on his desk and got up slowly. He was not old, but he moved like an old man.

Sally led him to the churchyard where the leper was waiting close to the wall, as crouched and quiet as a hare. She knew there was no need for her to come but she wanted to hear the voice again.

The leper talked with the priest. He explained that he had come a long way and was going to continue on his journey, so there was no need to be afraid that he might be a burden on the village. But before he went he wanted something to be done for him. He wanted the priest to perform the Service of the Burial of the Dead over his living body.

'I have been told it would make this sickness of mine easier to bear,' he said in his soft voice. 'I have the black cloth with me in my sack and I know the procedure. We could do it now if you are willing.'

The priest nodded his acquiescence. He took the cloth from the sack and went into the church.

He reappeared carrying the silver cross that was used for Saint's Day processions. He told Sally to hold the cross and lead the way. The leper followed through the arch of the door under the smiling mermaid and the priest came last, chanting as he walked, '*Libera me, Domine*. Master set me free.'

Two wooden trestles had been set up at a little distance from the altar and the black cloth was draped between them. The leper knelt before the cloth while the priest sprinkled holy water over him. He bowed his head and shuffled forward on his knees until he was under the cloth. The priest continued with the recitation of the Mass while Sally stood to one side and watched what was happening. Her baby did not cry.

Once the service was completed they went out into the churchyard. The priest dug up a spadeful of loose earth and sprinkled it over the leper's feet.

'Now you are in the grave,' he said, 'buried as well as dead, just as you wished. I hope it brings you peace.'

Sally and the priest accompanied the leper along the road until they reached the boundary stone that marked the end of the village. There were so many questions that Sally wanted to ask and yet could not. Who was this stranger and why had the sickness chosen to fix itself on him? Where did he come from and where would he go now? Would he live alone in some wild place like the hermit who lived in the forest, or would he go to a leper house? There was one not so many miles away and if he was there then Sally could visit him. She could show him how the baby was becoming a child. She suddenly dreaded the idea of losing this man as well, so soon after finding him. But she didn't speak, she walked in silence.

Before leaving the leper rummaged in his sack. He took out a bundle wrapped in silk and a few coins from his purse. He placed these gently on the ground.

'The money can pay for prayers for my soul,' he said to the priest. 'The book is for you,' and he turned towards Sally.

For a moment Sally thought she might see the face within the hood, but she saw nothing more than the eyes which swam towards her from out of the darkness like fish.

Already the leper had turned and was setting off down the road, his wooden boards clacking as he went.

The priest picked up the coins and put them in the pocket of his robe. He picked up the bundle, unwrapped it and revealed the bound pages of a little book.

He examined it carefully. 'It is a guide for travellers to the Holy Land,' he said. 'It describes the journey to Jerusalem and tells you where you can stay and what you can expect to see in the places you pass through.'

Sally took the book in her hands. The pages were as smooth as silk and they rustled slightly as she turned them as if they were alive. In the corner of one page there was a delicate brown stain and she could just see the thin lines of veins that had once carried the movement of the blood on this part of the animal's body. It was like a miniature tree or the skeleton of a leaf. The person who had written into the book had avoided touching the mark, as if it was dangerous in some way.

Sally looked at the words that had been flattened onto the pages like squashed insects. How could it be possible that marks such as these were the description of a journey? How could they contain the way to go, the dangers to be avoided?

She began to cry because of her ignorance, the book still open in her hands. The priest took it from her. 'Look,' he said, 'here is a map.'

He unfolded a double page and spread it out for her to see.

'Here is England,' he said, pointing at a ragged

shape. 'You must follow this red line over the sea which is blue, until you reach the country called Holland. You go through other countries as far as the city of Venice, and then the line takes you by boat around the edge of what is called the Great Sea, until you have reached the port of Jaffa. And here is Jerusalem. And that building must be the Church of the Holy Sepulchre.'

Sally stared in amazement at the shapes that were countries, criss-crossed with lines that were roads and lines that were rivers and surrounded by the rippling waves of the sea. In the blue water she saw that there were ships and mermaids, whales and other fishes. On the land there were churches and castles, a wild man covered with hair, a unicorn and some other beast which she could not recognize. She hoped to find her father, somewhere close to the red line, but she could not see him.

The priest folded the map and handed her the book. She tucked it securely under the cloth that bound her baby close to her.

That evening when the baby was sleeping, she placed the book tenderly on her lap. She breathed in the musty smell of it. She licked the words in case they might taste of anything she knew. Without really considering what she was doing she tore off a small corner of the map and put it into her mouth. She chewed it until the skin was quite soft and then she swallowed it.

She ate the map entirely. It satiated her hunger for a while and it made her feel as if she now contained the knowledge of distant lands growing inside her like a new baby.

Eleven

Time has passed, winter has moved into spring. The red-haired girl is walking through a bean-field.

The sweet scent of the bean flowers make her feel dizzy. She sits down abruptly on the side of the path. She traces circular patterns with her finger in the pale dust. She watches a line of ants moving with great purpose from one side of the path to the other. She becomes aware of the hum of bees and as she looks up at the sea of flowers all around her she realizes they are like insects too, with white petal wings surrounding a scrabble of black which could easily be mistaken for an insect's body.

She breaks off a beanstalk that leans over the path and picks one of the flowers to suck the drop of nectar it contains, the sweetness tugging a thin line through the inside of her mouth. She examines the two tiny bunches of beans just beginning to take shape, the shrivelled remnant of a flower clinging to each green tip like the umbilical cord of a newborn infant. She eats them and they taste as pale and delicate as their own colour.

She gets up and continues walking, her head throbbing now with the rhythm of her heartbeat. She walks over the smooth brow of the hill and down towards the village, following a track hedged with cow parsley that leads directly to the church.

When she reaches the gate into the cemetery she pauses under the shadow of a huge yew tree. It was said to be the first tree to grow in this area after the waters of the Flood had receded. There is a solemnity about it which must come from the things it has witnessed over the succession of years, beginning on the day when the land for miles around was covered with the stinking drowned corpses of those killed by the anger of God, through plagues and wars, harsh winters and long summers, up until this present moment when a red-haired girl is gazing into the clustered darkness of its branches.

The girl enters the cemetery and pauses by the fresh earth of her grandmother's grave. Once again she can see her grandmother lying in a coffin on the floor in the house, her mass of grey hair still somehow alive even though her face was empty of the person who had once inhabited it.

Some people linger after they are dead. You can feel them peering in at a window, sitting quietly in a chair, moving through a deserted garden. Others are impatient to be gone and they leave no trace behind. The girl's grandmother had been like that; it was as if there was nothing to hold her, nothing in the world she wanted and so she had quickly turned her back on it all and walked away.

The girl continued to sleep in the big bed she had shared with her grandmother, but every morning she would wake up before the lifting of the dawn with a sense of utter desolation that leapt out from the ambush of the night in the moment when she remembered how alone she was.

She had grown accustomed to looking at the old woman's face and seeing something of herself reflected there; listening to the old woman's laboured breathing and being reassured that she was herself alive. Now she was cut off from this sense of her own existence, floating in a space with no visible boundaries, no recognizable landmarks.

She stares down at the grave and wonders if her grandmother could even be persuaded to return to the village on the Day of Judgement. Was it possible to be so preoccupied with other things that you failed to hear the sounding of the trumpet? And even if she did come back along with all the others, a great bustling crowd of them shoulder to shoulder, bursting out of the earth, then would the girl be able to recognize her? The priest had explained that on The Day they would all be thirty-one years of age, even little babies and the very old. They would all be fit and healthy, even the ones who had been torn apart by an accident or some terrible illness. The girl could suddenly see herself moving desperately through that crowd, going from face to face in search of one that was familiar to her.

People change so much with death. When Sally found her husband washed up on the sand close to where the mermaid was buried, the sea water had turned him into a different person, his body white and soft. Sally had not been convinced it was him until she saw the ring on his finger. She had insisted on putting shoes on his swollen feet before shutting the lid of his coffin. She said he might be confused after all that buffeting in the waves and if he was wearing shoes then at least he would be ready to step forward as soon as the angel called out his name. The swelling would have gone down by then so his feet would not cause him any pain in the tight shoes. 'He will be as he was,' said Sally and the priest had nodded his head in agreement.

Now the red-haired girl remembers that young man's feet and how helpless and fragile they looked;

quite different to her grandmother's which were as hard and dry as firewood and seemed closer to a tree than a person.

She pauses as she walks into the church by the east door. The man with leaves in his hair hangs from the corner of the roof and stares down at her. His big hands tug the sides of his mouth wide open and his crouching body seems ready to leap forward like a huge frog.

And there is the mermaid, her fat fish legs spread wide above the arch of the door and a look of lechery on her face as she smiles to reveal a row of pointed teeth.

The red-haired girl is in the church and the dim underwater light is all around her. The air smells of stale urine because in the winter the children like to piss against the big stone pillar over by the bell tower; grown men do as well sometimes, but not the women. You can see the crystals of dried piss glinting on the floor when all the candles are lit.

The girl looks at the picture in the stained-glass window. An angel covered in feathers is telling the Virgin Mary that she will soon bear a child. The angel's face is filled with compassion and the girl feels his eyes meet hers across the immense distance that separates them and she is strangely comforted.

Someone puts a hand on her shoulder, gripping

tightly at the bones beneath the skin. She turns to be confronted by a man she has never seen before. Instead of speaking he sticks out his tongue, which is very pointed and wet.

He wraps her into his arms and she lets him take possession of her body as if it belongs to him by right. She doesn't even cry out or protest when she feels a brief stab of pain in the pit of her belly, but lies quiet and limp on the floor with the weight of the man pressing down on top of her and the cold stone eating into her back.

After the man has gone she remains there, drifting through something which is neither waking nor sleeping. She seems to be buried under a deep layer of earth and she can see the white threads of the roots of plants all around her.

Without any particular sense of surprise she becomes aware that she has turned into a bean: a smooth, kidney-shaped bean. From far away she can feel the strength of the sun pulling at her through the earth. With a great effort she moves towards it, bunching her bent knees under her chin and clasping her arms tightly around them. A white root grows out of her belly and lodges itself into the earth beneath her, while a green shoot wavers up towards the light and the air and the sunshine.

And then the sensation has passed and she is once

again nothing more than a young girl with red hair lying on the stone floor of a church. There is a smell of piss in the air and the colours coming in through the stained-glass window are dappled like flowers all around her.

She gets up and leans against the pillar before going out with cautious steps into a day that is still hot and bright. A thin line of blood is trickling down the inside of her leg and she rubs it away with a handful of grass.

She wanders into the village, pausing in front of a house from which comes the sound of a baby crying. She walks in and there is Sally sitting in a corner gutting fish. Her baby is gripping her skirts, trying to steady himself and crying with the frustration of the effort, but when he sees the red-haired girl he lurches towards her on bow legs, crowing with delight. She catches him in her arms before he falls and kisses him, breathing in the smell of skin and hair. And in that moment she decides that she will live here, with Sally and the baby.

Twelve

Every night Sally dreamt the same dream in which she found her husband swept up onto the sand, his hair matted with seaweed. And as she crouched beside him trying to find the courage to touch him, he would open his eyes in a lazy intimate way as if he was lying close beside her in bed. He would stretch out his hand towards her and explain in a languorous voice that he was not really dead.

'I held my breath,' he would say. 'I held my breath while the waves turned me over and over and tried to pull me down. And I floated and floated until I was able to come back to you. I am sorry I was gone so long.'

Then with a sigh he would release his held breath so that a fountain of water erupted from his mouth. And Sally would wake filled with relief because he was alive, only to realize once again that he was after all dead and cold and buried in the churchyard. She had put shoes on his swollen feet. She had wrapped him in a shroud. She had sat beside him through the night singing to him as if he was a restless child, and she had gone with the priest and the people from the village to bury him after he had lain in his coffin for three days.

Now the red-haired girl slept with her in the bed. The baby slept between them. The moonlight shone silver through the window, covering them both with a pool of shallow water. Sally searched for something of her husband in her baby's sleeping face, but she could find no trace of him there.

The red-haired girl always lay on her belly, the flames of her hair spreading out across her back and shoulders. She had begun to look after the baby as if he was her own.

Sally was indifferent to this change. Her one emotion was her sense of loss which made her feel like a stranger in her own life and her own body. She longed to escape from this present time but she could not see a way.

On this particular night, when she woke from the repetition of her dream, she clambered from the bed, careful not to disturb either of the sleepers.

She picked up the book which the leper had given her and stepped outside. It was dark but the darkness was made visible because everything – the houses, the trees, the road, even the line of the horizon – was covered with a thick, colourless layer of moonlight.

She was startled by a noise that sounded like someone muttering curses close to her feet, but it was only a hedgehog grumbling to itself and busy with the search for food. It disappeared under the shelter of a bush on stiff legs, rustling last year's leaves as it went.

'I must go and see the priest,' thought Sally. 'He won't mind that it's late. He told me he often works through the night. He could talk to me, comfort me, read my book to me.'

And so she walked through the silent village until she reached the priest's house. It was a small building, more like a hermit's cell, built onto the wall of the churchyard.

The door was open and Sally could see a glimmer of candlelight inside. She entered as quiet as a cat and settled herself into a shadow in the corner.

The priest was sitting at his writing desk, the candle flickering in front of him. His back was turned, but Sally could see the side of his face when he bent forward over his work.

There was the scratching of the goose quill on the sheet of vellum and every so often he spoke softly to himself. 'There now,' he kept saying. 'There now. There now,' as if this was a part of the process of putting the words down and fixing them in their place.

He paused to rub his cheek with his hand and Sally watching him could feel the roughness of the stubble under the palm of her own hand. He sighed and bent forward again, holding the quill poised above the page so that Sally licked her lips and tensed her whole body from the effort of concentration she shared with him.

She stood in the shadow for some time until she grew tired and then she left as silently as she had come. The priest turned to glance over his shoulder when she was no longer there. Although he had not been aware of her presence, he sensed her absence.

However, he did see her when she came the next night. She was bolder now, hypnotized by the process in which words were being hatched by a moving hand in the stillness of the night.

She was standing right beside him, and at first thought she was an angel dressed in a white shift and staring at him with an intensity that was like hunger. Then he realized it was Sally.

'What do you want?' he asked. 'What have you come here for?'

'I am so sad I don't know what to do,' she said in a matter-of-fact voice. 'I would like to go away from here, but I am not able to. I thought if you read to me from my book, it might help. But what are you writing now?'

'I am copying the Book of Revelations,' said the

priest. 'The Book of the Revelations of Saint John the Divine. I have just reached the pale horse with Death riding on his back. There now,' and he withdrew the hand that had been shielding the page.

'Where is the horse?' said Sally. 'Will you show him to me?'

'Here,' and the priest took hold of her finger and steered it to a mark that hardly looked any different from all the other marks.

Sally stroked the horse. 'Will he stay there for a long time?' she asked, as if it might be swallowed into oblivion by the same magic that had created it.

'Oh yes,' said the priest, 'it will stay. I make my own ink. Oak apples from Aleppo. Iron salts from Spain. Gum Arabic from Egypt. It will stay.'

He took the goose quill, dipped it into the ink horn and gave it to her, showing her how to hold it with the two middle fingers and the thumb.

With a shaking hand Sally made a tiny insect mark on a scrap of vellum. The ink turned from blue to black as it dried.

'What have I written?' she asked.

'Nothing as yet,' said the priest, 'but I could teach you. We could use your book. We could begin with the map. We could look at the pictures on the map and the words that go with the places and in that way you would learn to recognize the sound of the letters.'

'But I have eaten the map!' said Sally and she could feel her face hot with shame. 'I wanted to be able to go to Jerusalem and I thought if I had the map inside me then I could find the way!'

The priest could see this girl with her gazing moon face eating the image of a mermaid, a castle, a river, a boat. He could see her eating cities and countries and entire continents as well as the ocean which lapped against their shores.

'Maybe you will be able to find your way now,' he said.

After that Sally often went to the priest's house during the hours of darkness when her dreams had woken her. She sat and listened to him reading from the book and slowly the images of far-away places took shape within her mind and she travelled with the priest's voice further and further from her home and everything that was familiar to her.

The priest taught her how to write her own name and the name of the holy city of Jerusalem. When she put these two words together side by side she felt she had written the story of a long journey.

Thirteen

On one occasion after Sally had gone, I stayed there in the room with the priest, watching the concentration on his quiet serious face and the poised movement of his hand as it formed new letters and words on the page before him.

After a while, he rose abruptly to his feet and went over to a bowl filled with water standing in a corner of the room. He bent his head to gaze at the wavering reflection that confronted him. He saw a very tired face, haunted by doubt and anxiety. He had not realized until this moment how old he had become with the passing of the years. He let out a yelping cry as if the teeth of a trap had caught hold of him and he slapped the palm of his hand hard against the surface of the water, making the fragile image disintegrate.

He was suddenly aware of how little experience he had of the world. He had witnessed love and desire, pain and fear as it swept through the lives of others, but nothing had ever touched him directly. He wondered if he had decided to join the priesthood because it enabled him to listen to the confession of sins he would not know how to commit, to speak to the sick and dying with words that to him offered no comfort. People thanked him for the prayers he wrote out for them but he doubted if they ever worked in the way they were meant to; the mermaid had returned to fetch Sally's husband and he blamed himself for that. He longed to hear the voice of God whispering in his ear, or to be accorded some vision of eternity that would alleviate his feeling of desolation, but although others had told him of what they had heard or seen, he feared that for himself even in the hour of death he would be alone in a silent place.

And now he had agreed to go on a journey for which he was totally unprepared. He had never considered leaving this village where he had been born, he was afraid of making a sea crossing and he dreaded entering countries where he would be a complete stranger. His one scrap of comfort was the thought that Sally would want to go with him; after all the idea planted itself in her mind when she ate the torn pieces of the map.

But before he could go he wanted to know what lay ahead of him and that was why he decided to visit the hermit who lived in a cave somewhere close to the shrine of Saint Anselm. The hermit had been to Jerusalem. He had crossed the Great Desert and had lived there with the heat, the silence and the solitude. Surely he would be able to tell the priest what to expect from such a journey.

And so the priest set out for the shrine, following a path that went through the forest and ran close to the meanderings of the river. I was there with him, now at his heels, now at his side, now lingering, now waiting as he approached. The may trees were already in flower, their mass of tiny petals falling like snow on the ground and floating in drifts on the flowing water. There was the voice of the cuckoo. Toads were mating in the soft mud of a ditch, each pair clamped together like a single, two-headed creature.

Sometimes the priest was startled by the sound of his own footsteps, the rustle of long grass or the gentle crack of a twig, but although he glanced furtively over his shoulder, he knew that he was on his own and far from other people.

The smooth trunks of the birch trees were like the torsos of naked bodies and their branches were arms locked in a tight embrace. The passion of the trees unnerved him.

He approached a tree with a single overhanging branch that served the purpose of a gallows. The body of a young man was dangling from it, stirring in the breeze and giving the impression of awakening life although the sweet stench of putrefaction surrounded it like a high wall. The priest looked up and saw a man as young as he had once been himself and he stumbled and almost fell in his haste to pass by.

When we reached the shrine of Saint Anselm a number of people were gathered there, waiting for a miracle of one sort or another. A man whose legs had been broken in an accident had been brought in a wheelbarrow and laid out on the ground with his twisted swollen limbs close to the golden casket that contained the saint's thigh bone.

Two brothers were shackled together with a chain around their necks, having come from a distant city to do penance for some terrible crime. They had covered the last stretch of the journey on their knees and now they sat side by side, nursing their torn skin and their bruises and muttering a stream of urgent prayer.

A woman whose menstrual blood had not stopped pouring from her for more than a year, was standing waist-deep in the river, her skirts pulled up and the water around her stained red.

A man who was said to be as violent as he was mad had been strapped to a plank of wood and carried to the shrine in a bullock cart. Now he and the plank that held him were propped against a tree and he was staring open-mouthed at the casket as if he saw within it the possibility of reason and escape.

But it was the hermit whom the priest was seeking and he found him easily enough. His home was a hole cut into the river bank and he was sitting beside it, basking in the sunshine.

The hermit was filthy. His cloak was stiff with dirt and so were his long beard and his straggling hair. His skin was cracked and broken and he had rotten teeth. He was talking to himself in a nasal, high-pitched voice while scratching and twitching and searching his body for vermin. He smelt of excrement.

The priest approached in trepidation.

'Aha!' said the hermit. 'I see a man of God!' and with that he began to laugh, but the laughing made him cough and the coughing made him spit.

'I have come for guidance,' said the priest humbly.

'Of course you have,' replied the hermit, 'and I have it here for you.' He rummaged under his cloak until he had found what he was searching for and with a magician's flourish he produced a small dried hand, severed at the wrist.

'This,' he said, waving the hand from side to side, 'this is the hand of the blessed anchorite Saint Anthony who lived alone in the deserts of Sinai. Here is your guidance.' And he presented it to the priest.

The priest took the hand. It was hard and smooth

and very reptilian. It looked as though it would be quite capable of hopping across the hot sand, pausing to eat, scurrying into a hole for safety. The fingers and the thumb were clasped quietly together, giving the impression that the whole thing was asleep.

'Thank you,' said the priest, at a loss for words.

'My pleasure,' said the hermit, smiling to reveal the stumps of his teeth. 'I was with the saint in a cave for many years. His lion was there as well and it slept beside me, as warm as a woman. I took the hand as a remembrance.'

'What else can I say?' said the hermit. 'Bones,' he replied almost to himself. 'Collect them. As many as you can find. With or without the skin. I had a basket filled with the fingers of Holy Innocents but I lost them in a storm at sea. And I had all the teeth of John the Baptist, but they went as well. At least I got Saint Anselm's thigh bone and brought it here. When the shoemaker's wife threw it into the river they said it was gone for ever but I searched for it and found it caught in a branch. It's safely back in its casket and now the river water performs miracles as well. It's very good. It cures anything from nostalgia to the sweating sickness. I sell it in bottles.'

Suddenly the hermit lunged forward and grabbed the priest's hand, pressing his sharp nails into the palm. It was an act of such violence and intimacy that the priest was horrified. He wrenched himself free and ran towards the safety of the forest, chased by the hermit's high-pitched laughter.

He ran until he was exhausted and then he lay down among last year's bracken with the trees whispering over his head. He noticed that he was still holding the saint's hand in his own. It was as dry as old bread with hardly any weight to it. He put it in his pocket.

And that was all. On the following morning he set off back home, but I was no longer with him. I had already returned to the village under the cover of darkness.

Fourteen

While the priest was making his slow way back through the forest, Mary, the woman who saw devils, was almost killed by her husband. Some people in the village said it was the priest who saved her, but the priest said it was Saint Anthony's miracle and not his.

I remember the first time that I caught a glimpse of Mary's husband. He was there beside her in the room with the devils and although his face was turned from me I could feel the rage inside him like a rat in a box. I tried to warn Mary, to tell her what would happen next and how she must escape quickly, but she didn't hear me.

She had changed a great deal since the day when she was tied down on the big bed with the manacles chafing at her wrists. She had seen the air around her thick with golden floating angels, and after that there were angels everywhere. They rose and fell within the shafts of light among the trees. They surged towards her in the mist that rolled in from the sea. They sang to her, they talked to her, they told her their secrets.

Sometimes she would look up from whatever she was doing and one of them would be gazing at her solemnly from across the room. They were all similar in the way that they were neither young nor old, neither male nor female, but she learnt to recognize some of them and they told her their names. Gabriel and Ezekiel were her favourites. They smelt of honey and burnt cedar wood.

The angels formed a ring of protection around her. They encapsulated her in a world of her own where she was no longer burdened by sadness.

Before she had always resented the loneliness of her childhood, the unhappiness of her marriage, the death of three of her children and the arrival of the devils who had turned her into nothing more than a thing, to be stared at and pitied. But now she accepted it all. She even accepted her husband and she was no longer afraid of him in the way that she had been.

She continued with the usual pattern of her life but her character had changed. She never stopped smiling a secretive private smile and she would often pause to listen to words that no one else could hear. Then she would nod her head in agreement and even laugh out loud so that her shoulders shook and tears came to her eyes.

She no longer wanted to sleep in the big family bed with its heart and its unicorn, its dead and living children, its forgotten lovers. Instead she went into the barn and made a nest for herself in the hay. She enjoyed hearing the breathing of the cow and the rustle of rats and mice as they raced across the high roof beam or over the floor. An owl lived in the barn as well, but it flew on such silent wings that it never disturbed her.

Her husband watched her. He followed her wherever she went and while she was sleeping in the hay he would take a lantern and come to stare at her there.

He was full of strange fancies. 'You are the Angel of Death,' he said to his wife. 'And I am Michael who stands at the gate and weighs the souls. Some of them are yours and some are mine. We must fight.'

Mary his wife looked away and said nothing.

'You pretend to be a saint,' he said, blocking his body in front of her so that she was trapped in a corner. 'But I have the power to see what lies inside of you. I can see the filthy snakes in your belly.'

The shoemaker's wife overheard him. 'You must do something,' she said to Mary.

'But there is nothing to be done,' Mary replied.

One night while she was lying in the barn, her husband came as usual to stare at her. And when she sighed and smiled in her sleep he took her neck in both his hands and began to shake her violently from side to side. He was screaming.

Mary opened her eyes and saw his wild mad face close to hers. 'Either I am going to live or I am going to die,' she thought to herself.

Her body was limp in his hands. He knocked her head against a wooden partition, tightening his grip around her throat. She felt tired and empty but unafraid. There was a roaring sound inside her skull getting louder and louder.

In the same instant when the balance seemed to have tipped irrevocably against her, she caught sight of a very old man standing just behind her husband.

He was not one of her familiar angels, he was much too old for that; but neither was he a devil. He had a long white beard and eyes that were so unnaturally bright it looked as though stars were shining through them. His skin was as dark as a chestnut and it was hard and scaly and wrinkled, like the skin of a lizard.

'Perhaps he is an Ethiopian,' thought Mary, who had never seen anyone with a skin of this colour before. 'Or one of the Three Kings. The black one who brought gold.'

The old man's head was tilted to one side like a

thrush listening for the movement of worms under the ground. Then with a sudden ferocity that didn't belong to his extreme age, one of his hands shot out and grabbed Michael by the shoulders. This hand was a small and compact thing which seemed independent of the body that owned it. It swooped down hard and tight with the energy of a water bird diving for fish.

Mary felt the hold on her throat softening and she realized with a vague sense of surprise that she was going to live. She lost consciousness and tumbled into a quiet darkness that welcomed her but did not threaten to keep her for too long.

She woke to find that she was back in the family bed with the priest sitting beside her. At first she thought he was the angel Ezekiel or perhaps the angel Zacharias, the two of them could be so easily confused. But angels always wore white and had the golden dish of a halo above their heads. This man was dressed in a black robe and she recognized the priest.

'Are you in much pain?' he asked.

Mary put her hands to her throat which was bruised and swollen. She ran the tips of her fingers around the sockets of her eyes and they felt hot and soft. 'No,' she said. 'There is nothing wrong with me. But where is Michael, my husband? He was here.'

The priest told her that as he walked into the village he had seen Michael with his legs in the stocks. They were new stocks and they had been made in such a way that a person's legs were hoisted quite high so that it was difficult to move and impossible to sit up. It would be very uncomfortable in the rain, but the weather was dry.

Michael was left there for several days. People made sure that he had water to drink and they gave him a little food. They had seen the bruises on Mary's throat and the dark rings around her eyes and so they guessed what must have happened.

The priest looked after Mary until he was sure she was strong again. He told her about his visit to the hermit and showed her Saint Anthony's hand which he kept safe in his pocket. She noticed how hard and dark the skin was and how it was covered with a patina of thin lines like a spider's web.

She thanked the priest for what he had done, but he said he had not really done anything; he had come after it was all over. He gave her the hand as a present and she was glad to have it. She used to place it on her lap and stroke it as if it were a cat. She felt sure it would protect her from any further harm.

Fifteen

Once the shoemaker's madness had passed, a different level of closeness developed between him and his wife. He would stare at the intimacy of her face and in the lines around her mouth and eyes and across her forehead he could understand and accept that he was growing old. The whiteness that was creeping over her soft hair delighted him for its unexpected beauty. The pleasure he took from the sexual act was quieter and yet more profound; it was like dying, but without the fear.

The two of them went walking hand in hand. They followed the raised path that separated the land from the sea further up the coast. They climbed among the high sand dunes that were gathered there in great rolling waves, breaking and falling in silence and immobility.

They settled themselves in a sheltered hollow on the side of a steep bank from where they could look out over the North Sea. Striped dragonflies were whirring sleepily in the air. The water was a uniform and almost transparent grey, with the shadows of clouds shifting across it. They saw the dark back of a whale emerging briefly in the distance like a newborn island.

'The whale is the largest of God's creatures,' said the shoemaker, picking up a handful of fine sand and letting it run silky between his fingers.

'Yes,' said his wife, and although they didn't say anything more they were both thinking about the occasion when a whale was brought ashore in a storm. It lay helpless and gasping on its side and everyone from the village gathered around to watch it with a mixture of fear and pity. And impatience as well, because they were all hungry and they would hack it to pieces and eat it as soon as it was dead.

The shoemaker's wife remembered how the whale's eyes were brown and sad and could have belonged to a cow. The shoemaker saw again the pink and ragged scar that cut across its body close to the tail, and he wondered if it was the same creature that capsized the old fisherman's boat, leaving him clinging to its useless shell.

A tuft of coarse grass was growing close to where they were sitting. The shoemaker saw a glittering object lodged among the sharp leaves but when he reached out to grasp it something stabbed him or bit him and with the sudden rush of pain he withdrew his hand.

'What was that?' asked his wife.

'I don't know,' he replied, sucking the palm where the hurt lay.

His wife parted the grasses and nestling among them she found a grey worm with a round black shiny head like a little seed. 'It must have been this,' she said, picking the worm up between her finger and thumb and throwing it away.

She examined her husband's hand. There was a tiny puncture mark and a drop of blood, but nothing else. 'Does it still hurt?' she asked.

But her husband was lost in thought. He stared out at the sea. 'It will pass,' he said and smiled at her. There was a coating of sweat on his upper lip and his face looked suddenly exhausted.

They walked home slowly, the shoemaker leaning against his wife's shoulder and concentrating on each step he took. Neither of them spoke.

That night he became ill. His wife wished she had not thrown away the worm because if she had kept it she could show it to the woman who knew about such things and she might have helped with a cure. A grey worm with a black head had bitten her husband, and that fact could not be undone. You could never tell where danger was coming from or who it was going to strike next.

The shoemaker talked continuously while the fever raged through him and his body was hot and wet. His wife did her best to follow the racing of his mind. 'The clock,' he said, and she realized he was referring to the big clock they had seen on the tower of the cathedral. 'Oh I wouldn't want to live near a clock. That long metal chain pulling down the minutes and the hours, step by step as if it was measuring the length of life itself. I watched the clock. I had never seen such a strange thing before.'

'I was there too,' said his wife. 'I went there with you to the city. We watched the clock together.' But her husband did not seem to hear her or at least he made no sign that he did.

'When the King of France died in battle,' he said, speaking more quickly now with the heat racing over the surface of his body like a fire spreading across a field of dry corn, 'they boiled him. In a pot. They buried his cooked flesh there where he had fallen with an arrow through his heart. But they put his clean bones in a box and sent them to his wife. So that she could have them. And remember him by them. Her King.

'But I don't want to be boiled in a pot. Ask the priest to bury me. Inside the church. I would like that.

Under the floor. Close to everyone I know. Listening to you all talking together. Hearing the approach of your feet. Knowing that you think of me when you look down and see my name written on a big flag-stone.'

The shoemaker's wife tried to calm her husband. She held him in her arms, glad for the familiar smell of him.

The shoemaker talked in his fever about his blindness. 'I was afraid when the scales fell away from my eyes,' he said. 'I felt as if I had been flayed alive, the skin peeled from my body. I had no protection. I was so cold! I am so cold now as well!'

His wife held him while his body burned.

He talked of his madness and how his tears would not stop falling. 'Hold me! Please hold me!' he said with desperation in his voice because he could not feel the pressure of her embrace even though she held him with all her strength.

By the morning he was quite peaceful. The fever had left him and his body seemed to have shrunk to half its size. He kept running a hand across his face to reassure himself of his own existence.

'Do I look strange?' he asked his wife.

'No,' she replied, but this was not true. He looked as if he had seen a ghost and was seeing it still.

Shortly afterwards a storm passed right through

him, shaking him with such a force that his wife thought it would kill him in the way that a bolt of lightning can kill a man.

He never spoke again, although he often hummed a particular tune, over and over, very softly.

He couldn't dress himself or feed himself or look after any of his basic needs and so his wife did it all for him. Her children had grown up and he had become her new child. She loved him with the same patient love she had felt for him from their first meeting.

Throughout the weeks that followed he would sit in front of the fire watching the flames. He hardly ever slept and so his wife kept the fire burning during the night as well.

When his trousers were soiled she would change them, endlessly busy with the task of washing and drying and coaxing him to eat small morsels of food. He followed her with his eyes and fretted the moment she was out of his sight.

Sometimes in the evening she would sit next to him by the fire and he would lay his head in her lap and suckle from her dry breast.

When it was obvious that he was close to dying she asked the priest to come. She explained that her husband must be buried under one of the heavy stones on the floor of the church. That was his wish.

'He doesn't want to be shut outside in the rain and the cold,' she said.

The priest agreed, even though there had been a terrible stink of corpses in the church during the last hot summer and whenever possible he persuaded people that it was better to be buried outside in the graveyard.

He had brought a book with him called *The Art or Craft of Dying Well* and he showed it to the shoemaker's wife. It contained illustrations of the stages of death: you could see the dying man in his bed being visited by grieving members of his family, by devils who reminded him of his sins and threatened him with damnation and by angels who reassured him with the promise of eternal life. The last picture in the book was of the soul escaping from the body and rising towards the ceiling of the room. The shoemaker's wife looked at this image carefully and then held it in front of her husband's face so that he could look at it as well.

'Death is a going out of prison and an ending of exile,' said the priest.

She nodded her head in agreement but kept her eyes fixed on her husband. 'He will miss me,' she said. 'I don't think he minds dying, but he will miss me. And I will miss him.'

The priest gave the shoemaker a crucifix to hold

and he held it tight while gazing at his wife with tenderness and longing. He seemed to be about to speak, but he died without saying anything. His wife kissed his eyes closed just as before she had kissed them open.

After the priest had gone she sat there next to her husband. She thought about the song she had heard him humming to himself during these last weeks. It was a dirge that people sung during the three days of waiting before a burial takes place. It told how the soul needs to go on a journey over an expanse of waste land. This land is covered with thorny bushes, but if the person has been generous to the poor and has given them the gift of shoes during his lifetime, then he can now have shoes to protect his feet.

He travels until he reaches the Ship of Death, with flames pouring from its sides, but if he has given the gift of milk and meat to the poor during his life, then the flames won't hurt him.

The shoemaker's wife sang for her husband and as she did so she could see him setting out across a wide flat land on which cruel thorn bushes were growing. She saw him putting on a pair of soft shoes that he had made himself.

Then the Ship of Death reared up before her eyes. She held her breath as she watched her husband pass quite close to it, but he was not hurt in any way. She thought she saw someone coming forward to meet him and welcome him but she could not be sure. She wished that he might turn his head one last time to say goodbye, but he did not.

Several men from the village lifted up one of the big yellow stones on the floor of the church and dug a deep hole beneath it. The coffin was lowered in and covered over. The shoemaker's wife went to the church every day to kneel on the stone. She imagined her husband looking up at her from where he lay. She stroked the letters of his name.

And then one night when she was sleeping and missing the warmth of his body even as she slept, he spoke to her in a dream. 'You must go to Jerusalem,' he said. 'The priest and two others will be going as well. I will come with you for some of the way, until you can manage on your own.'

She went to the priest as soon as it was light to tell him what she had learnt. She liked the idea of travelling to a strange country.

Sixteen

Autumn, winter, spring and summer. A year had passed, the seasons had come full circle and now it was September again with a low sun casting long shadows across the land.

Everyone in the village was filled with a sense of impending dread. They knew that the approaching winter was going to be very severe because there were so many warning signs. The geese were flying off in great creaking crowds even before the month had come to its end. The trees were much too heavily laden with fruit, anticipating that they couldn't presume to survive and so had to trust in the scattering of their seeds. There was a feeling of time itself closing in, of a gate being clanged shut while the world waited with growing apprehension.

Then the oldest inhabitant, a man who usually never bothered to speak a word to anyone, suddenly began to talk and talk with the urgent inspiration of a prophet.

'It began just like this,' he said, his voice sticky with age, his sunken eyes flickering as they searched for what they were looking for, settling on distant remembered images as a fly settles on meat.

'The Great Pestilence began just like this, but we didn't know what was coming because it had never happened before. The geese flew off too soon. The trees had too much fruit. Then the cold came. Birds dropped frozen from the sky. Fish died, animals died, people died in their beds. The sea close to the shore was covered with ice, cracking and splitting with the waves and the movement of the tides.

'Winter passed but there was no spring at the end of it. Storms flooded the land, tore up trees, smashed boats and houses. We planted seeds but they never sprouted. We had no crops, nothing to live on.

'The sun remained hidden behind a thick grey curtain which hardly let in any light. A big ship drifted into the bay and was caught on a sand bank, tipped helplessly on one side. Some of us managed to get to it in a boat and we found the deck covered with the blotched and swollen bodies of dead men.

'But one man was still alive. He told us how he had travelled through France and Italy and had seen terrible things. A thick stinking mist was spreading over the land, killing everything it covered. A pillar of fire was burning above the Pope's palace in Avignon. Clouds of locusts were falling dead in the fields, ankle deep. Earthquakes swallowed whole villages. Some women saw a river of blood surging towards them. They ran from it screaming and others joined them until there was a huge crowd. They reached the cliffs by the sea but they didn't stop and they were all broken on the rocks beneath or drowned.

'And now,' said the old man, 'I can feel it coming back as it was before. We didn't learn and we are being punished again. There is no hope. It will be the end of everything.'

When he had finished speaking he made a dark rasping sound like a raven. He looked like a raven as well with his black cloak, his wicked flickering eyes, his dangerous mouth.

He died shortly afterwards. The priest sprinkled a great deal of holy water over the shrivelled corpse and he was buried quickly with no family or friends to weep over him.

People began to see signs everywhere. A robin was found lying dead on the altar of the church and no one had the courage to remove its tiny frozen body. The mermaid could be heard singing under the ice-bound sand and her voice was sour and threatening.

At the convent one of the nuns began to mew like a

cat. The sound took possession of her and even when she was beaten with a stick she could not be silent. The contagion spread among the other nuns for a while so that they all mewed and cried together in one piteous chorus, but then it stopped as abruptly as it had started.

The cold became so intense that people could hardly speak, hardly move. They sat in a hibernating silence and grew thin.

A few men from the village gathered enough energy to go to the priest to ask him what was the cause of this punishment and what could be done to lift it. But although before he had always had some words of prayer or explanation, he was now at a loss. He sat in bed with his shoulders hunched and a cat sleeping across his knees. The room was hardly more protected than the world outside and it had no fire burning in the grate.

The priest didn't bother to look up when the men entered and he made no attempt to answer their questions. 'I want to go, but I don't know the way', he kept saying to himself and when they shook him and asked him to explain what he meant he said they should go to Sally, she might know the way because she had swallowed the map.

The men could not understand what the priest was talking about, but nevertheless they struggled through the snow to where Sally was living with the red-haired girl and the child.

They stumped into the kitchen and stood there, shifting their feet with their heads lowered like cattle, their breath steaming.

When Sally appeared pale and subdued from the other room, they crowded around her. She felt the danger in their presence. She felt how they might close in and trample her to the ground.

'You have to do something,' said one of the men and the others muttered in agreement. 'The priest said you knew the way to save us. He said you can do something because you have eaten the map. You are our only hope.' And again there was a muttering and a sense of threat growing stronger.

'I don't know what I can do. I don't know what the priest thinks I can do,' said Sally, 'but I will try.' With that she wrapped herself in a heavy cloak and with a blanket around her shoulders she went out of the house, walking in the direction of the sea.

When she got within sight of it the wind was so fierce she could hardly breathe and she had to lean forward against it just to keep herself upright. Great swathes of sand were being blown along the beach and the sharp grains bit into her exposed skin and stung her eyes.

She stood and stared towards the line of the

horizon, searching for something that would offer reassurance and comfort. Far away within that uncertain distance she seemed to see a whole crowd of human figures waving and calling to her. There was her mother and her father and so many others she had lost and missed over the years and there finally was her husband, beckoning for her to come back into the warmth of his arms. All she had to do was to break through the battering of the wind and then she could run until she reached that other place where they all were. That surely would bring an end to the grip of cold that had trapped the village and everyone within it.

I saw her standing there, tiny and frail, doing battle with the elements. I saw the effort she was making and how at last her strength failed her and she fell to the ground.

I thought she would die and when a figure dressed in black appeared and scooped her up in his arms I thought it was Death come to get her. But as he turned towards me, carrying the limp body, I saw it was the leper.

He took Sally back to the village. He pushed open the door of her house and laid her down gently on the floor in front of the fire.

The red-haired girl removed the blanket and the cloak and dressed her in dry clothes. Her little son came and sat beside her. The men from the village were still gathered like a herd of cattle in the room and they watched what was happening.

When Sally opened her eyes again it was evening and the light from the fire was dancing on the walls. Many more people had come by now and they were all waiting for this moment. As soon as they saw that she had returned to them the leper said, 'Now I will tell you about my travels and how I was healed of my sickness.'

The thaw started once he had begun to talk, the sound of his voice interrupted by the sound of ice dripping from the eaves of the house and the soft thud of snow as it fell in heavy lumps from the roof and from the branches of the trees.

Seventeen

Looking back I can see now that I was spending more and more time in the village simply because I did not know what else I could do, where else I could go. I was so empty I could have been blown across the land like a leaf; so lost, I had no idea how to begin to find my way back to some sort of quiet. The one thread that held me was the knowledge that I could always enter that other place in that other time. I was not made welcome there, but neither was I told to leave.

I became very ill. A sense of utter exhaustion had invaded me and I could feel it spreading through my body, coursing with the blood in my veins. I could not fight what was happening because I had no energy with which to fight. It was not that I wanted to die, but I would have welcomed the chance of ceasing to be, at least for a while.

And then I suppose I could have died. The days

and nights became merged into one endless babble of time. Until at last I was taken into hospital for an operation.

I lay in a strange trance waiting for the anaesthetic to take effect. Everything around me was white: white curtains, white walls, white sheets, even the garment I had been given to wear was a stiff bright white cotton.

The anaesthetic was drifting through me like smoke and then it began to become heavy like water, pulling me down into itself and the secret of its own oblivion.

But as I sank and surfaced and sank again within the whiteness that surrounded me, I turned to the leper. I saw him with Sally and all the others from the village. He was telling them the story of what had happened since he left and how it was that he had come back again. His voice rose and fell in a rolling monotone and behind it I could hear the muffled drip of melting ice, the soft thud of heaps of snow falling to the ground.

I was there in a dark room lit by the dancing flames of a log fire. I could smell the salted herrings that hung in a bunch from a hook on the ceiling. I could smell the sweet resonance of hay, the cloying sweetness of excrement and rotting vegetables, the sharp stink of urine and the pervasive musty odour of damp and slow decay.

The room in which we were assembled was

breathing and shaking like a living thing because of the battering of the wind outside. I knew that these walls were made from a mixture of cow dung, horsehair and lime. There was a cat's skeleton hidden within the blackened tower of the chimney and next to it a pair of leather shoes, small ones for a child. Rushes cut from the reedbed were spread out on the floor and they felt slippery under my feet.

I could hear the restless activity of rats and cockroaches and two thin cats going about their business and I could just distinguish the outline of a broody hen sitting blank-eyed on a pile of old rags in a corner. A little boy sidled up to me and climbed onto my lap. He fell asleep as abruptly as a door closing. There were lice moving through the tangles of his hair.

The people around me shifted and changed like fleeting shadows when I tried to see them all together in a group, but if I concentrated on them one by one their faces slid into focus and I could recognize them individually and remember everything I knew about them. The whole village seemed to be gathered here, even those who I had thought were dead and gone.

The leper was telling his story and his words were becoming more clear to me now that I was growing accustomed to the sound of his voice. He had reached the port of Great Yarmouth and he had just persuaded the captain of a ship to take him on board in return for a large sum of money. He agreed to keep himself hidden throughout the journey because the other passengers must not see him. I suppose a member of the crew would bring him food under the cover of darkness.

The ship was carrying pilgrims to Finisterre on the north coast of Spain, from where they intended to walk to Santiago de Compostela. But it never reached its destination; there was a storm which swept it against a rock and shattered the hull.

Everyone was drowned except for the leper who was carried miraculously ashore and washed up on a sandy beach. He lay there face down, stripped of his clothes, his body twisted into a loose curl.

'I was found by an old man and an old woman,' he said. 'They thought I was some sort of sea monster because my skin had turned white and ragged from being soaked so long in the water, making me appear more like a fish than a man.

'The woman took hold of my shoulders and rolled me over onto my back. She saw a flicker of life in my eyes and even though they were afraid of me, she and her husband fetched a handcart and brought me home to their house.

'I was weak and helpless and they looked after me as if I was a baby. They fed me on goat's milk and dressed me in loose clothes that wouldn't hurt my skin.

'Every day they would strip me naked and rub my body all over with oil and then they would carry me into the sunshine and leave me with a cloth tied over my eyes so that the brightness would not hurt me. I lay in a sort of trance, the sun, as it felt to me, munching into my skin like a caterpillar on a leaf.

'At first I resented being found and cared for in this way. I felt it would have been better if I had drowned with the others or if I had died alone on the shore like a stranded fish.

'I tried to fight my despair by remembering how I had been before the sickness disfigured me, so that I needed to hide my face and warn people of my approach. But all I could see was a tiny distant figure lost in the landscape, a stranger who would not come close.

'Then I let my despair sweep over me and I drifted, passive and inconsolable, while the old man and the old woman moved me from sunlight to shadow and back into sunlight again.

'As the days passed I began to be aware that the outer surface of my body was changing. My skin was becoming tighter and tighter. It gripped me and held me like a metal casing and I thought it would kill me, but then it began to split and tear and fall away in thin ragged patches.

'I could only see what was happening to my hands because I was always dressed in loose robes when I was brought in from the sun and the blindfold was removed. But my hands, which had been pock-marked and covered with a white mildew of sickness, were now pink and smooth. It looked as though they had been burnt by the flames of a fire, but they were healthy.

'I decided that if I was completely healed, then I would go on a pilgrimage to Jerusalem. I had once been as far as the gates of the city and I had seen something of the desert that lay beyond it. I wanted to return, to tread in my own footsteps for a second time.

'And because the change in me had begun in this village I thought to come back here as soon as I could. I felt sure that the priest and Sally would come with me, and perhaps others as well. I knew that this was the place from which I must set out.

'Slowly my entire body grew smooth, until I no longer needed to be rubbed with oil and laid under the sharp gaze of the sun. I began to go walking in the mountains. It was a beautiful land, harsh but beautiful.

'The old man and the old woman had been

watching over me as I grew from childhood into manhood, all within the space of a few weeks. When they saw that I was cured they knew that they must lose me. They wept and embraced me but made no attempt to persuade me to stay.

'Before we parted we set out to Santiago de Compostela where the body of the Apostle James was brought after he was washed up on those shores in a stone boat.

'The three of us walked up the steps of the cathedral and knelt to kiss the bare feet of the statue of the saint and the heads of the two lions on which he was standing. We went inside and sat by the tomb where he was buried. I put my hand through a hole in the stone of the tomb so that I could feel the hard flesh of the body of the saint. Then we parted and I made my way back here.'

The leper was silent and there was no sound of breath or movement in the room.

With my heart beating like heavy wings inside my body and my mouth so dry that I could hardly move my tongue to form the words, I spoke to the leper. My voice wavered and fluttered in the air and I doubted if he would hear it.

'I would like to see how you have been healed,' I said.

Without a moment's hesitation he pulled back the

hood which still covered his head and concealed his face.

'Here I am,' he said.

I walked through the thick crowd of people and stood in front of him. By the light of the fire I saw that his face was covered with a swirling pattern of scars, but there was no sign of any sickness on it.

I said, 'If you are going on a journey then I would like to come with you. I would like to see Jerusalem and the deserts that lie beyond it. I would like to be one of your companions.'

Eighteen

As I finished speaking I felt the weight of the anaesthetic pulling me down and down until I had lost the leper and the people who were with him and there was nothing left to see or hear or hold on to. Even the dizzy whiteness of walls and sheets had dissolved and disappeared.

Time passed and there was no way of measuring it. When I finally floated back to the surface of the world I knew that the threads which had been holding me were cut. I was ready to leave the village.

Everything I had grown accustomed to would soon be changing. I was going away and once I had gone I could probably never return even if I wanted to. In the silence I could hear the methodical thump of my heartbeat and the gentle inhalation and exhalation of my breath.

And so, over the days of convalescence while I lay

in bed and drifted in and out of sleep and wakeful-
ness, I began to say goodbye to the place which had
been like a home to me for over a year. I walked as
slow as old age along a road that was imprinted in my
mind. I stood and gazed with a lingering tenderness at
the line of crooked houses which had offered me
shelter when I needed to escape. I peered wistfully
through windows and open doors.

A few of the rooms were occupied by men and
women and children, but most of them were already
empty, with broken ceilings and rubble on the floor.
Nevertheless they were all still redolent of the stories
they held and in each contained space I could see the
memory of the people who had been here and the
lives they had lived.

This process of valediction was sometimes joyful
and sometimes painfully sad, but there was nothing I
could do to stop it from following its course. Although
the thaw which had started while the leper was telling
his story had by now melted most of the snow, the
weather was cold. The sky was a clear transparent
blue and there was no wind.

I made my way past the church and the yew tree
and down to the rickety hut by the shore where I had
sat with my back to the wall on the first day that I
came here. Once again I felt the crunch of shells
breaking under my feet and when I looked out

towards the horizon where the air and water merged together in a shifting haze I was brought as near as I could ever be to a sense of eternity.

Further along the coast I could just distinguish the wavering line of the sand dunes where the shoemaker and his wife had sat together among the whirring of dragonflies. In the other direction there was the flat expanse of muddy sand and a black stone marking the place where the mermaid's hair was buried. The little boat in which the old fisherman had set out across the North Sea was pulled up on the shingle, tilted to one side, its nets spread out to dry.

I knew that whales, porpoises, mermaids and sea monsters were to be found in these grey waters that I would soon be crossing. Unicorns, wolves, hermits and wild men covered with hair were in the woods, the mountains and the uncultivated waste lands. An angel could be recognized from the way it glittered, a devil from its stench and the sound of grinding teeth. Death was out roaming at his leisure through all the three elements and a person must fall down like mown grass as soon as they heard him call them by name.

A clump of samphire was growing among the pebbles beside the hut and I bent down to break off a stalk that was as tight as a drum, the thin skin tinged pink and orange. I bit into it and the salty liquid it contained tasted like my own tears.

There was nothing more to be done. I had arranged to meet my companions at the boundary stone and as I approached I saw that they were already there: Sally and the shoemaker's wife, the priest and the leper, standing in a huddled group and waiting for me.

We all looked curiously alike, enveloped in grey pilgrim cloaks, the hoods decorated with the red cross of Jerusalem. We each carried a strong walking stick, a purse of money hidden close to the body, a bag for food, a bottle for fresh water, and a sack with a few simple possessions.

Only a handful of people from the village had come to witness our departure. The red-haired girl was there with Sally's child perched on her hip, his head almost lost within the mass of her hair. The woman who saw devils was peering at us from behind a tree, her face distorted by a mad smile that kept breaking out into laughter. The shoemaker appeared out of nowhere just in front of me and stared fixedly over my shoulder and towards his wife. I knew it was a throng of ghosts, but I would miss them all.

No one spoke or waved as we set off but the dog with pale eyes followed us from a distance, his tail between his legs and his movements furtive from the habit of avoiding sudden blows. A thin rain had begun to fall and I heard the dip dip dip cry of a woodpecker, answered by the fierce shriek of a jay.

We were walking together in silence, busy with the realization of departure. We passed a field where the tiny spikes of young wheat were just breaking through the earth and then a meadow where three brindled cows stood under the shelter of a huge oak. A weasel raced out in front of us and for a few seconds it forgot its size and vulnerability and reared up on its hind legs to threaten us, swaying to and fro like a snake. Then with a flick of energy it was gone into the long grass beside the track.

I was next to Sally, our steps swinging with the same rhythm. She had never left the confines of the village before and now she walked like a bullock being led to slaughter, her head bowed and her mind closed to anything beyond the thudding contact of her feet with the ground, the swishing of her cloak, the weight of the long staff in her hand.

When we stopped at midday to share a meal of hard-boiled eggs, hard cheese, hard bread and stale beer, she ate what she was given but refused the beer, preferring to drink from a nearby pool. The water was sweet and brackish and it coated the inside of her mouth with the taste of mud and rotting leaves. The monotonous cry of a bird sounded like someone calling out for help, her child perhaps, or was it her father or her husband? It was only now that she was leaving the village that she was able to understand how much she had lost during the last year and how sad she had been.

As evening approached we reached a barn and we spent the night there with the darkness immense outside and the rustling of rats in the straw. Sally was so restless that it was hard to know if she was awake or asleep. She whimpered like a little child, the noise so close and intimate it sounded like my own voice.

Nineteen

I want to try to put words to the shock I experienced when we entered the first town on this journey. It was the port of Great Yarmouth, the same place from where the leper had set out when he was bound for Santiago de Compostela. There was nothing particularly extraordinary about it, it was a town like any other, but I had no idea of what to expect.

We had passed through a forest of beech trees, their bark as smooth as skin and moss green. Then we had followed a raised track that took us safely across an area of marshland. The colours on that marsh were so startling: dark reds and greys and purples interspersed with patches of water glistening like liquid mercury. And the birds. I had never imagined such a quantity of birds. They were a thick restless carpet on the land and rushing clouds of movement in the sky. I can still hear the noise of them: burbling songs, harsh screams, the creaking of wings.

The walls of the town emerged out of the mist like a monstrous face with gates for its many mouths, through which people streamed in an endless flow, and towers for eyes, the narrow windows staring down to judge those who approached.

We joined the crowd that was heading for one of the gates and we were swept along with them and into the town. People shouted and pushed around me and there was a savagery in their determination which allowed no time to pause, no room for mercy. I caught hold of Sally's hand when I stumbled on the uneven cobblestones and I kept it in my grip as if I would drown without it.

The houses lowered at me and the streets between them were dark and narrow. There was a beggar lying in his own filth, the corpse of a dog, a heap of rags, a jumble of bones, a piece of broken chain and then we were suddenly tipped out into the light and space of the market square.

All the shops around the square were hung with signs to explain their trade. A surgeon had a wooden arm painted with dripping stripes of blood, a barber had a long sharp knife, a tavern had a bunch of branches tied together like a broom and leaning out so low that it brushed against the top of my head.

Above the cacophony of sounds I thought I could hear someone screaming in agony, but it was only a pig being slaughtered. I saw it stretched out on a trestle table, its skin pink and human, its throat cut so that the head lolled in a final ecstasy and the belly slit wide open and steaming into the air.

Two women were busy washing the pig's entrails in a tub of water. They laughed contentedly as they squeezed excrement out of the long tube of the intestine and one of them managed to throw a length of it around a man's neck as he walked past. It dangled from him as fresh as an umbilical cord and that made everyone roar with laughter.

People were selling things from little stalls set up on the paving stones. Chickens, tied by their feet and suspended from hooks, stared at me with amazement. Tethered goats shifted and bleated uneasily. There was dark bread, a few vegetables and lots of fish.

A stone cross marked the centre of the square and wooden stocks and a metal cage had been erected just beside it. I blundered against the side of the cage and thought at first that it contained an animal, but then I saw it was a man, shivering and naked, his body blotched with vivid colours from the cold, the dirt and the bruises which covered him. He was cowering on all fours in a corner.

'What did you do?' I asked him.

'I don't remember,' he replied.

The stocks held a woman by her wrists and ankles.

She was slumped forward with her face concealed by her hair. A few young children, who must have been her own, snuffled close to her, as piglets do when their sow is trapped in the farrowing pen.

The leper kept on striding ahead while the four of us scuttled after him. I still held Sally's hand in mine. Without it I might have tried to run away even though there was nowhere to run to.

We crossed to the other side of the market and reached the church of Saint Nicholas. The saint was standing by the door to welcome us. His cloak was bright blue, his cheeks were bright red, his hair was bright yellow. In his hands he was holding the severed heads of three children. Behind him was the painted barrel in which the children's truncated corpses were soaking in salty water. The saint was poised right on the edge of the miracle that would restore the heads to their bodies and bring the children back to life. I saw that everyone who went into the church knelt to kiss him, congratulating him for what he was about to do. His wooden cheeks and the hem of his wooden cloak were shiny from the touch of so many lips.

We were not inside the church for long, but I did see the big ship which dangled from chains fixed to the dome of the ceiling and the spiderweb of wires which I was told were used every year when the Star of Bethlehem was made to whizz across the vaulted space until it hung, shaking with the effort, above the altar.

Then we were threading our way through more streets until again there was a sudden opening into space and light. But this time we had reached the limits of the land, with a view of a wide estuary and a river racing to meet the sea.

A pair of gallows stood on a wooden platform overlooking the water. Between them these two awkward structures were carrying the weight of twelve dead men. They hung together in an exhausted clump. There was something vaguely convivial about their companionship and something terrible about their isolation. They were so close to each other and yet so utterly distant from each other. They all had their heads facing the sea, staring with empty eyes into a far distance. The image hooked itself into my mind and often came back to me later.

Twenty

The sun was already setting as we approached a three-masted ship in the harbour. The leper spoke to some sailors and within moments we were ushered up the gangplank and onto the deck. I went to sit on my own because of the shock of the town and the dead men.

A pile of gutted herrings had been heaped up on the wooden boards and now that it was dark their bodies began to shine with a natural luminosity. When I stroked one with my finger it took on the same pale gleam.

That night I slept alongside the others under a canvas awning and among bales of oily wool with a stink so strong it rasped at the back of my throat. While the ship rocked and groaned across the waves I dreamt that I found Sally's husband washed up naked on the shore. He was wrapped in the mermaid's arms and she had two tails like soft legs which were snaked tightly around his waist. In the dream I sat beside their fused bodies and stroked the skin that was as rough as a cat's tongue and the skin that was smooth.

I was aching all over when I woke and I could not begin to imagine where I was or why the ground beneath me was heaving with so much movement. I thought the sickness must have returned, bringing with it the nausea and the dizziness and the sense of being marooned on a raft, salt on my cracked lips. It was only then that I remembered what was happening; how I was leaving one place and going to another.

I clambered out from under the shelter of the canvas. It was broad daylight. The leper and the shoemaker's wife were nowhere to be seen, but Sally was with the priest and he was reading to her from the book of travels to the Holy Land. I wondered about the map which Sally had swallowed and whether we would be able to find our way without it. I could imagine it floating in the darkness of her belly: roads and rivers and oceans, mountains and valleys all jumbled up together and the red line marking the direction we must take, broken into little pieces.

The priest turned a page of the book and the thin vellum rustled as if it still belonged to a living animal. I could just distinguish the pinprick marks where the hair had been growing and the delicate ridge where the skin had stretched tight across the line of the vertebrae.

'Where are we?' I asked Sally, but although she looked towards me she didn't hear me. She was trapped in some quiet labyrinth of the past, searching there for what she had lost. And so it was the priest who answered.

'We have crossed the North Sea,' he said, 'and we will soon be entering the port of Zierikzee in Holland,' and with that he pointed towards the outline of a tower standing guard at the harbour entrance. The people who were gathered on the quay to watch us had square-tipped fingers and big-boned faces. Their voices were thick and rough, angry in their strangeness although there was no anger intended. They led us to an inn and we sat around a table in a low-ceilinged room. A plate of smoked eels was set before us. They writhed together in a motionless heap, their mouths gaping.

I was next to the priest and I could feel how the rolling of the waves had not left his body. He had a slight fever and that made the eels smile at him, twitching their slippery tails. He felt as exhausted as someone who is recovering from a long illness and without waiting to eat he excused himself and made his way to the sleeping room.

This room was lit by the embers of a fire glinting in

126

the hearth. It contained twenty or more beds and many of them were already occupied. The priest moved between them, feeling for the outlines of bodies with his hand. When he found one that was flat and empty he pulled back the rough covers and lay down. Insects bit at his naked legs and his belly but he was too tired to notice them.

Somewhere quite close to him there was the sound of a man and a woman lying together, the wood of the bed creaking with the rhythm of their bodies. The priest remembered the warning in the leper's book, 'Beware of inns,' it said. 'Beware of inns and of women who try to persuade you to enter them. Such women are all common prostitutes and they will rob you or even kill you.'

The wood stopped creaking and then it sounded as though the two people were dying with a single exhalation of breath. The priest had never shared such a sense of intimacy before.

He wanted to pray, but instead of prayers all that he could remember was the list of strange words he had been learning from the leper's book. 'Offena, kis-zones, meela, betzim, daegim, elohim, zatan, eyscha,' he said, surprised by the authority contained in the unfamiliar sounds. And that meant: a ship, a shirt, an egg, a fish, the Lord, the Devil and a woman, although he was not sure what country the words were from.

Sleep came to him finally, and as he slept the fever fell away. I was lying beside him. He smelt of wax and honey. His hair was soft against my lips. He did not dream.

We set out again in the morning, walking through a blanket of mist that merged with the camouflage of our cloaks so that we were hardly visible to each other. We followed the hugeness of the River Rhine: a sweep of turgid water, flooded meadows, windmills grinding their teeth into the wind and willow trees cut back so that they resembled a line of clenched fists.

I can see us now, walking along a road day after day, our feet tired and blistered and often bleeding, with rags to bind the wounds. Walking along a road like migratory birds. Moving steadily southwards and only dimly aware of the softening of the weather, the shift from marshland to forest from forest to mountain slopes.

I remember how in a church I saw Christ riding on a donkey and his naked feet were tipped and strained upwards so that he could keep his balance on the animal's back. You could see the tension and the effort involved from the way the bones and the sinews were revealed.

In that same church there was Saint Vitus who cures people suffering from epilepsy, the bite of a dog or a snake or a spider, and the many other forms of madness. He was bending his neck under the sharp blade of a sword that had already drawn a few drops of red blood and the words of a prayer were escaping from his mouth like a swarm of bees. He was peering out at the world from between strips and swathes of cloth that had been draped in dirty curtains around him.

Not far from that church we heard the sound of bagpipes and drums and shrill whistles carried in the air. And then we saw a hectic crowd of people growing louder and drawing nearer. Everyone here was caught in the same net which turned them into one single lurching, reeling, dancing creature. Their faces were blank and shocked and uninhabited. I could see fear hopping among them, pecking at the glint of an eye or the glitter of a ring.

One woman at the centre of the crowd was spinning with her arms stretched wide as if she was trying to spin herself out of this world and into some other. Her belly was terribly distended and strips of cloth had been tied tight into the flesh to relieve the pain it was obviously causing her.

The priest went up to the woman. He wanted to comfort her, but all that he could offer was the incantation of words from the book of travel. A ship, a shirt, an egg, a fish, the Lord, the Devil, a woman. Offena, kiszones, meela, betzim, daegim, elohim, zatan, eyscha. It sounded like a prayer of enormous power. The woman fell quiet and the crowd fell quiet with her.

The priest led the way back to the church. He took the woman to stand exhausted in front of the saint, the bees of his prayers buzzing around his head. And as we watched we saw the madness that had inhabited her slip like snakes out of her mouth, her nostrils and her ears and fall hissing and writhing to the floor. Then the priest slowly unwound the long cloth that had been pulled tight across the woman's belly and he hung it up, stiff with blood and dirt, alongside the others that were already hanging there.

Twenty-one

Looking back now I realize that I was moving from one of my companions to the next, shadowing them in turn and following them with the same furtive longing as that dog with pale eyes which had first brought life into the village for me.

During the early days of our journey I had hardly spoken a word to the shoemaker's wife, hardly even noticed her presence. But then walking behind her I became aware of the steady rhythm of her body. I could see her small feet in their worn shoes with the toes clenched and the skin of the heel cracked and broken. I could feel the weight of her breasts lolling together in a casual intimacy, the sweat trapped beneath them. Her belly had been stretched and slackened so many times by pregnancy and birth that it was marked with rows of white scars like little knife wounds.

Her back was slightly hunched and there was a

thickening of flesh and muscle where the neck joined the shoulders, as if something of the stubbornness of her nature had concentrated itself there. Her neck was often painful when she woke in the mornings, but then the pain shifted and was quickly forgotten.

Even though her body had grown tired she knew how much more difficult such a journey would have been when she was still bleeding every month. A bundle of rags stiff with dried blood chafing at her thighs, and when there was no blood then the inevitable stirring of a new baby in her womb.

She would often talk to these babies as they grew inside her, becoming fond of them long before she saw their crumpled faces. The one she had felt closest to was the one who had emerged with a huge slack mouth like some creature from the sea bed. He only had a few moments to stare at her with eyes as grey as winter and then he was gone. Her husband had cradled him, not realizing he was dead until he touched the cold fish mouth with his lips.

Her husband was often with her, but then she had never doubted that he would be. On the first night after they had crossed the sea, he hammered on the door in her dream and burst into the room, hugging her so tight she could hardly breathe.

'Can you feel how I am holding you?' he said. 'Can

you feel how my body presses against yours? Oh, I am so hungry!'

And then he had taken her hand and stroked it across the curled hairs of his belly so that she could understand how empty it was.

'I will feed you,' she said to him and she put her face close to his and opened her mouth wide like a bird feeding its young so that he could plunge his head inside her and find food.

He was walking beside her now on the road, his step synchronized with hers. When she looked up she saw that we were passing through a great forest of oak trees as powerful as an army of saints or the massed souls of the dead. Their bark was thick and broken and bubbling with old age. Some had been struck by lightning, leaving nothing more than a burnt-out shell of wood, and yet their branches were decorated with sprigs of pale young leaves and the ground was littered with acorns.

You could find signs of animals everywhere: patches of deep loose earth where the wild boar had been rooting, the stink of fox, the sharp footprints of deer or bison and occasionally the presence of some dark shape watching with fear or hunger from among the shadows of the trees.

I so much wanted to talk to the shoemaker's wife. I wanted to ask her about her life and how it appeared to her when she looked back on it. Had she been happy, even during the time when her husband was blind or when he was crying? How did she see her future now that he was dead and could only visit her in the silence of dreams? Would she choose a different path to follow if she could go back and begin again and would that path still find her here on the road, walking?

But before I had the opportunity to speak there was the sound of branches crashing and cracking in the undergrowth and something staggered out from among the trees and stood balanced on two hind legs, swaying and panting in front of us.

It was a creature shaped like a man but covered in shaggy hair like a wild animal. The hair was dark and matted with broken twigs and last year's bracken. The features of the face were hidden in every detail except for the grey staring eyes.

Which was when the hunters came. Two dogs as delicate as hares ululating their delight in the chase and two men on horseback following at their heels. Between them they cornered their quarry against an oak tree and one of the men threw a net over him, tangling him into it. He made a deep bellowing noise and I'm sure that I heard him cry out, 'Mercy, mercy, mercy!' but no one listened to him. A spear was rammed through the mesh of the net and into his heart.

We watched because we could not stop ourselves from watching. The men dismounted and got the body free from the net. They took out sharp knives and they began the work of slitting and pulling until they had removed the covering of skin like a heavy garment. Then we all saw without any doubt that this was a man they had killed, red and shining.

The shoemaker's wife came forward. Sitting beside the corpse, she took the head in her lap and she began to cry. The authority of her anguish made the dogs and the men move back. She was crying for this particular death but she was also crying for her husband's blindness and his tears and how she still missed the warmth of his body night after night. And all the time she gazed with pity and tenderness at the naked wild man, as raw as a wound.

When finally she came to the end of her lament, she stood up quite practical and matter-of-fact, drying her eyes and blowing her nose and pushing back the loose hair streaked with grey. 'Shall we go on now,' she said quietly, 'it's getting late.' She placed herself between me and Sally, like a horse in the shafts of a cart, and we set off once more.

We spent the night at an inn called The Three Kings. We ate roasted stork which tasted bitter and pungent. We slept in goosefeather beds that swallowed us into their clinging heat. Over breakfast a man who was taking mineral salt and bales of linen to Venice offered to give us a ride in his cart drawn by two oxen. We settled ourselves among the sacks and bundles. The cart made such a noise as it rattled and juddered along the road that it was impossible to think, let alone try to speak.

The air became colder and more thin as we entered the foothills of the Alps. Trees were replaced by grass and then by rock and scree and the first scatterings of snow. A tiny spike-horned deer darted like a lizard across a steep rock face. Big eagles floated in the sky. The mountains that had looked as insubstantial as clouds in the morning light, now appeared solid and menacing.

There was a toll gate by the narrow pass that crossed through the barrier of the mountains from one side to the other. We all clambered down from the cart and went to pay our money to a man who took it without speaking or smiling, his hand closing over the coins and vanishing them into a deep pocket.

The larger of the two oxen was taken out of harness and tied to a length of rope and then with its head bowed in submission and its feet treading carefully, it led us one by one between the high banks of snow and ice. Occasionally it would pause to smell the snow as if receiving information about which areas of fragility were to be avoided. We were told that should the animal make a mistake then we must quickly let go of the rope before being pulled down into whatever danger had been revealed.

As the shoemaker's wife went through the pass she knew with an absolute certainty that she would be making this crossing only once; she would never retrace her steps. The realization made her feel very light-headed, as if she had been drinking wine in the clear air.

The road took shape again as we began to slip and slide our way down into a more southern world. We passed meadows with cattle grazing and the stretched branches of vines. I will never forget my first sight of the black flickering flames of the cypress trees, held up against the blueness of the sky. A cloud shifted to one side to reveal a glistening lake in the depths of the valley.

The leper turned to me just after I had seen the lake. The pale gleam of his scars shadowed by the grey hood was like the reflection of sunlight on water.

'So you are here after all,' he said. 'I thought you might be.'

Twenty-two

The leper was sitting so close to me that his shoulder was leaning and moving against mine. I could feel his heart beating within its cage of bone, the way his hands always shook no matter how he tried to steady them, the stretched tightness of his skin.

'It's different for me, coming here,' he said and his words were as quiet as my own thoughts so that I could not be sure if anyone else heard him. 'You see, I am returning home. I was born in Venice and I presumed I would live there all my life. But then I lost someone I had loved and I needed to escape to some distant country until the pain of my sadness had blurred and shifted and become less of a burden to me.

'I set out as a pilgrim bound for Jerusalem but before I reached my destination the sickness came and turned me into a leper. I had to wander among strangers for a long time. But now that time is over. Soon I will be treading in the footsteps of my own past and I will be able to see how much I have forgotten over the years and how much I still remember.'

Even as he spoke the leper could feel the familiarity of the landscape creeping up on him from all sides. They were following the banks of the River Agio which feeds the lagoon surrounding the scattered islands of Venice. Big mosquitoes were whirling like noisy haloes above his head and their bite was as sharp as ever.

At the edge of the lagoon there was a smell of salt water that was far older and sweeter than the smell of any other he had known since. It came to him like a first dim recollection of childhood. And then there was its soft milky turquoise colour and the sound of it lapping against the side of a pier and the leper could feel all the sleeping seeds of memory beginning to stir and stretch themselves in a single moment.

A rowing boat pulled up alongside the pier and the boatman smiled a conspirator's smile as the leper stepped aboard. 'So you have come back at last,' he said. 'Welcome.' His voice rustling like leaves, his teeth black, his breath musty from old wine. When the leper saw the lines of age which had grown on this man's face, he understood how long he had been gone. But he could not recall the man's name.

He sat down on a bench between Sally and the shoemaker's wife, while the priest and a woman whose head was turned from him sat on the bench opposite. He watched how the oars broke the water into shattered fragments of reflected light.

They passed those flat islands of mud and reeds that seem to float as thin as lily leaves on the surface of the lagoon. A flock of white egrets flew silently into the air, their wings wonderfully languid. A layer of mist clung around the boat, but the day was becoming clear and in the distance the sun was shining on the metal dome of Saint Mark's church.

And then the woman raised her head and the leper saw who it was. She nodded to him in solemn recognition. Her face was a mask of colours: white and red and black, carnival bright. The slippery cloth of her dress was tight around her breasts. She had not changed at all although the leper had forgotten the coldness of her expression, the transparency of her skin and the savagery of her, as if she had clawed feet within her shoes and scaly wings folded between her shoulder blades.

Seeing her now, the leper saw himself as the young man he once had been. He watched as she led him to a room in a house where the wooden bed was carved with curling patterns and painted with fresh gold paint. He felt her licking his skin and biting into his flesh with her teeth and her nails until nothing existed for him beyond the four walls of her being. But then, even as he stared at her, she turned away and vanished and Sally was shaking him and telling him to hurry because everyone was waiting and the boatman needed to be paid.

In front of him was the palace with its colonnades and balconies and the black and white tiles of the walkway were dizzy under his feet. And here were the two stone pillars marking the entrance to the great square, the one carrying Saint Theodore standing on the back of a crocodile, the other a golden lion brandishing a golden flag.

A metal bar was fixed between the pillars, with a dead man hanging from it, suspended by a chain. The fish market had its place at the foot of the pillars. The leper looked at the heaped fish and the limp man and he found them merging into one double mermaid creature in his mind: the scales becoming skin, the fishtail becoming human flesh, the cold becoming warmth.

He remembered the story of the mermaid who came to the village and brought such chaos with her and he felt he suddenly understood something about Sally and her sadness, which was close to his sadness in a way. And so he told her the story of what had happened to him long ago and how it had changed the direction of his life.

'I was accused of murder,' he said. 'The woman I loved was found floating dead in a canal. Everyone said I must have killed her. They wanted to make me confess to the crime and because I remained silent they removed the doors and windows from my house. It was a custom of the city. I had to walk in and out under the scrutiny of strangers. But I did not confess. I ran away.'

'And had you killed her?' Sally asked, her face blank of expression, making it impossible to guess if she also found him guilty.

'No, I don't think so,' the leper said, 'although I have gone over the events so often in my mind that I have become uncertain about what really happened, beyond the fact of her death and my unhappiness. I don't even know if we were still together as lovers, or if she had already left me before she died. All that I know is that she was gone and I remained.'

He began to walk more quickly, taking big strides as they crossed the square, so that Sally and the others were almost running to keep up with him.

They passed a church like a forest of tall trees and pushed through a crowd of men who were intense with talk and laughter. The smell of spices which he had almost forgotten. The vivid liquid colours of velvet and silk. A monkey chattering on a chain and then the woman's voice calling out his name, desperate with anger or despair. And there she was again, staring down at him from the window of a house, her long hair like flowing water.

Now faster than ever over three arched bridges, through a doorway and into a courtyard that was overhung with the leaves of a vine. Life-sized marble figures were grouped together in the dappled shadows like a welcoming party: naked men and women, a crouching lion with a human face and another creature with sharp wings and clawed feet.

The leper led his companions into this house which had once been his home. The rooms had high decorated ceilings and the sounds of the day came pouring in through the open windows. Everything had been left undisturbed, although the furniture, the books, the wall hangings, even the plates and glasses were muffled by a blanket of neglect which gave them a strange uniformity of colour and texture.

The leper said, 'When I lived here I kept an elephant in one of these rooms. It had been brought back from India. It ate pieces of cake from my hand, picking them up with the tip of its trunk which was as delicate and precise as a finger and thumb. But it missed its own country and died of nostalgia. I preserved the skull.'

Then he wanted to show them the skull as proof that everything he was saying was true. But although he searched meticulously throughout the house, he could not find it anywhere.

Twenty-three

The leper woke early and went out on his own into the city. The lagoon appeared red and solid in the dawn light. The clouds in the sky were carved into tunnels and deep caves of pink and grey rock. Everything kept reminding him of something else, the elements deceptive and the past breaking through into the present while the present sank back into the past.

He found himself standing on a wooden bridge and looking down at his shifting reflection in the canal. A loose tangle of rubbish was jostling between this floating image and the side of a rowing boat. He could see an empty bottle, a bunch of flowers, a broken piece of gold-painted wood and a little dog with black and white fur and the red gash of a wound on its side. One ear and the tip of the tail were still dry and somehow alert but the rest of the body had been pulled under the glaze of the water's surface.

And then he was seeing her just as he had found her: face down and naked, here or somewhere close by. He managed to turn her limp body over and for a moment he thought she must be still alive because he thought he saw a smile flickering across her face. But that was not so and she was dead.

He remembered running into the Rialto market-place. Wooden stalls were being set up and people were shouting to each other across the noise of their activity. A man dressed in a long blue robe brocaded in gold thread had pushed past him. The man was holding a little bag of spices to his nose to drive out the fetid stink of the city, and the leper had snatched the bag from him so that its sharp scent could spin through his skull like an avenging angel who can drive out any number of devils.

A group of prostitutes was gathered under the arched colonnades chattering together in starling voices. Two of them came lunging towards him, hand in hand and laughing. They were balanced on shoes with soles as high as three clenched fists and they kept slipping on the flagstones which were still wet from last night's tide. Their faces were sinister behind veils of thin black gauze. They tried to grab hold of him but he got away.

He passed a fish stall where a tangle of conger eels were pulsating in an earthenware basin, their mouths parted, their eyes grey and without mercy. Next to them was a stall selling hanks of long hair; they hung from poles like the tails of horses.

He went down a narrow street where the money changers sat hunched and silent in front of their shops and he bought some silver ducats which could be used as currency all along the coast of the Great Sea and some bills of exchange. It was a first gesture towards the need to leave this place and go to some other.

A street of tailors, cobblers and rope sellers. A street of jewellers. A man walking up to him, his breath musty from old wine; he realized now that it was the boatman, although he still could not bring back the name.

He went into a warehouse, the long building stretching back into its own darkness, and there he bought the things he needed for his journey: a mattress stuffed with sheep's wool, a duck-down pillow and a scratchy blanket smelling of cat's piss. He bought sausage, salted tongue and dried biscuit. Plague pills, seasickness pills and pills to prevent constipation. Wax and tinder, a game of chess, a chicken coop and a bag of corn to feed his chickens once he had them. A basin in which to wash his feet and a chamber pot for when the sea was too rough for him to reach the latrine on the side of the ship. A tin box with a good lock, a wooden flute, a white felt

147

cloak, a barrel of wine and two barrels for fresh water. He learnt later that thirst is a much more terrible thing than hunger, but he did not know that then.

The shopkeeper advised him to get a relic to protect him from storms and sickness and sudden danger, so he went into the next church he came across. The waxy marble of the walls on all sides was dancing with ghostly shapes and the waxy marble of the pillars shone like fevered skin. The floor was alive with coloured stones: onyx and malachite and agate; red marble, white marble and a pale green marble. There were the curling shapes of seashells outlined in some of the marble slabs and he saw one that was the same size and shape as a man's head, looking as soft as flesh even though it was sliced through hard stone.

The Last Judgement covered an entire wall. The Damned were crouched among flames which resembled sheaves of wheat and the Saved had wings bunched around their heads. In Hell there was a black pool in which floated the white bones of the dead. In Heaven there was a feathered angel, who stared at him across the distance that divided them with a look of compassion.

A priest appeared out of the darkness and showed him a whole jumble of saintly relics heaped up on the floor. Leg bones, arm bones, and fingers covered with shreds of skin. Skulls holding a few strands of hair or a little cluster of teeth. He bought himself a piece of the skull of John the Baptist, which the priest broke off for him like cake.

The same priest was still in the church now, but bent almost double with extreme old age so that he could hardly lift his head to look up from the whirling patterns on the floor. Nevertheless, he seemed to recognize the leper. He took him firmly by the hand and led him to the pile of bones. It had increased in size. The leper bought a fragment from a different skull of John the Baptist.

Then he returned to his house. He went from room to room looking at his companions who were all sleeping peacefully. The shoemaker's wife lay on her side, her face damp and flushed. The priest was propped on a pillow. His eyes were closed, and the weariness on his face had lifted, making him appear young again. Sally was sprawled on her belly, her back very white and smooth.

In the last room that he entered, the leper saw himself. He was lying in bed with the woman he had once loved wrapped in his arms and they were both fast asleep. For a while he sat down beside the two of them and the life which he had lost.

Twenty-four

What was it was like for the leper to come back, with the whole city haunted by the person he had been before he left, the things he had done and had failed to do while he was here?

Every bridge, every narrow street, every familiar building, even the enormity of the sky reflected in the lagoon, they all reminded him of what had happened in that other time. He could hear the stones of a wall calling out accusations as he tried to hurry by, the wooden construction of a bridge ordering him to stop and look at what lay beneath it, the water whispering the secret of his own doubts and fears.

He had returned and already he was desperate to escape a second time. This was not possible because, although there were two pilgrim ships tethered like horses in the harbour, neither of them was ready to leave. There was nothing for him to do except to wait and try to learn patience.

Everyone had a different reason to explain the delay. Some said that beyond the enclosed safety of the lagoon the Great Sea was so wild and angry it would smash through the hull of a ship within minutes, while the wind would strip every sail from the mast. Others said no, the sea was perfectly calm, the danger came from the pirates who were waiting in ambush around the islands of Dalmatia. There were also reports of plague with disfigured and bloated bodies of men and women and children, dogs and cattle, lying in heaps along the coast of Istria.

The leper's companions waited with him, but without his sense of urgency. They were unconcerned at the way the days rolled into each other and quite content to pass the time by wandering through the city. The leper took them to see the Doge's umbrella, the unicorn's horn, and the marble throne that had belonged to Attila the Hun. They went from island to island. They walked through churches and gardens and alleyways, through markets and shops. They entered the long dark warehouse which provided for the needs of pilgrims bound for the Holy Land and everything the leper had bought before was bought again.

He had hardly spoken while they were travelling but now he began to talk and talk. Wherever he went some new image from the past would break onto the surface of his thoughts and demand to be seen, and now instead of keeping these things to himself he told them to his companions,

They listened carefully but without comment. Sometimes he would describe a particular event several times, and with each new telling he became more aware how insubstantial his memories were.

Eventually the waiting came to an end and a white silk banner was unfurled in Saint Mark's Square, announcing that a ship was ready and passengers could go on board if they wanted to. So there they were, clambering up a rope ladder and standing on deck with all the others.

The smell of freshly painted tar. Smoke billowing from the charcoal fire in the kitchen under its canvas awning. The round staring eyes of sheep and cattle in one pen, the screams of a pig in another, beaks and broken feathers protruding from between the slats of a wooden crate crammed with geese and chickens. The oarsmen sitting at the benches where they would eat and sleep and tug at the weight of the water for as long as the journey lasted.

The leper recognized the captain and several of the sailors, the pilot and the soothsayer who worked together as a team, the scribe who carried his quill pen like a weapon and the ship's surgeon with his parchment skin and cold hands, always eager to play the part of torturer if the need arose.

Down five steps and into the dark, low-ceilinged space where the passengers must try to find sleep at night or during the day. Each one was allocated a small area on the floor and told to lie down. Then the outline of his or her body was drawn onto the wooden boards, marking the full extent of private territory. About a hundred would be sleeping here together, with heads pressed close to the creaking walls, shoes and buckets and locked boxes of possessions slipping and sliding and overturning with the movement of the waves. When the leper was last on board there were six horses stabled on the deck just above where his head lay, their hooves grinding into the bone of his skull, stamping and shifting through his restless dreams.

Someone lifted up the wooden hatch in the middle of the floor and a lantern was lowered on a rope to reveal the area below. Here sand was kept as ballast and the bilge water slopped from side to side and stank, no matter how often it was pumped out. You could bury eggs and wine and other things in that dank cold if you wanted to. The leper remembered how the body of a dead Venetian lord had been carried here for several weeks, the smell of him seeping through the floorboards and getting stronger and stronger so that even without seeing him it was easy to imagine his white flesh breaking into soft fragments and mixing into a paste with the sand and the water.

Back up onto the deck and the fresh air. The surface of the sea sparkling. A wind dancing. A big table had been placed next to the main mast and the scribe was seated behind it, writing out each passenger's details: name, country of origin, the fee which had been paid and what should be done with the possessions should the owner happen to die. When it was difficult to reach land for a burial then the dead were wrapped in shrouds and thrown into the sea. Only a very wealthy Venetian could expect the luxury of having his bones returned home. On the last journey ten men had died on a single night and there were not enough stones to weigh down their shrouded bodies, so they all bobbed to the surface of the sea and followed in the ship's wake for as long as they could.

The leper stood in line with the others, waiting his turn to answer the scribe's questions and wondering if he would be recognized. Suddenly the trumpets were sounding, shrill whistles were blowing and the main sail was unfurled to reveal a huge painting of Saint Christopher staring towards the horizon with black-rimmed eyes.

Seven white banners were flying from the rigging, each bearing a different image. The leper saw one that showed a lion representing the city of Venice and one that carried the red cross of Jerusalem.

The lead oarsman sang the opening line of a song and the others answered him in one voice as they raised and lowered their oars in unison, pulling the great weight of the ship away from the shelter of the harbour and out towards the open sea.

Twenty-five

The ship followed the line of the coast and always kept the land in view. The floodplains around Venice were replaced by the pale mountains of Istria; you could just see where geometric blocks of stone had been cut from the marble quarries.

They could not stop anywhere here because of the threat of plague. Twice they drew in close to a harbour town only to be confronted by an unnatural silence in the streets, lines of corpses laid out on the sand like a fisherman's catch, a few sad figures waving them away, or worse than that, standing like Death himself and beckoning them to come close and closer still to take a share of the desolation.

Within a few days the supply of fresh water in the barrels was beginning to taste sour. Instead of eating bread, lettuce leaves and olive oil for breakfast they had hard biscuits soaked in strong wine.

A bullock and a pig were slaughtered and the

sharks appeared miraculously on all sides of the ship as soon as the sea was tinged red with blood and offal. The sharks fought each other over the last scraps of food, their angry bodies cracking and slapping against the water's surface.

One of the passengers refused to leave the dank nest of his mattress. 'I am going to Paradise,' he said and he lay there drinking wine in the dark until he became as incontinent as a baby and the stink of him filled the entire space. Eventually he was lifted out onto the deck each morning and propped up somewhere in the shade where he continued with his talk of Paradise. And then he disappeared. He must have rolled overboard for the sharks to find him, but no one saw him go or heard him cry out. His possessions were given to the captain and his mattress was thrown into the sea. The space it had occupied was soon taken.

The passing of time was punctuated by the blowing of whistles and trumpets to announce the need to eat or pray, to rise or go to rest. When there was a fair wind the figure of Saint Christopher with his black-rimmed eyes was spread out against it. When there was no wind the oarsmen struggled to keep the ship moving.

Among the passengers there was a continuous babble of talk and laughter and sudden quarrel, the playing of musical instruments, the cheering and clapping when someone demonstrated the steps of a dance or how he could remain balanced on his head to the count of twenty. Above that was the sound of the sailors, who sang to each other to distinguish their voices from the general hubbub. They sang out instruction, reassurance and warnings of approaching danger. The oarsmen sang the rhythm of their oars and at night the steersman sang something like a lullaby, a little lilting tune that he repeated over and over as proof that he saw nothing to be afraid of.

Sometimes the leper would wrap himself into his white felt cloak and go and sit out on the deck all night long, listening to this song, watching the flicker of a single torch, the bright scattering of the stars, the sudden bursts of phosphorescence in the water. He felt empty of all emotion and curiously insubstantial, as if his body was nothing more than a thin shell that could be blown away with a single breath. His entire past life seemed as distant as some far landscape in which nothing could be distinguished beyond a vague outline of shape and colour. It seemed to him now as if many years had gone by since he left the city or even as if he had never been anywhere else but here on a ship in the night and there was no dawn to be expected to bring an end to it and no other place in the world apart from this one.

And when the dawn did come he would emerge grey and quiet from a listless eternity and go and join the others in the business of the day. But his companions noticed that he had become very removed from them and that he no longer told them any of the stories of his life. They watched him and wondered where his thoughts were taking him.

One morning the soothsayer and the pilot were seen in earnest conversation together. They both examined a map of the coastline that was covered with the tiny scratchings of fast currents and hidden rocks. They observed the way that the shadow of the mast fell across the deck and saw how a flying fish had landed sharp and breathless on the wooden boards just at the conjunction of light and darkness. That is what made them decide that it would be wise to stop at the next island which they could already see approaching.

And so the ship was brought into the shelter of a wide sandy bay. Some waited to go ashore in a little boat, while others were too impatient and waded waist-deep towards the unfamiliar luxury of land.

Everyone was eager to unwind their cramped bodies and they spread out quickly in all directions. Although there had been a fishing village here in the past and a few ruined houses bore witness to that fact, the island was known to be uninhabited.

A creaking chorus of frogs announced where there was fresh water. The ashphodels were in bloom, their fat bulbs lying haphazardly on the stony ground and their white flowers looking somehow cold and unskinned at the end of a long stalk. A cloud of bee-eaters flew into the air with sudden fright and for a moment they appeared like a rainbow of vivid colours. Wild sage was growing everywhere, its pungent scent released by the trampling of feet. There was also a small spreading plant called *porcella* with leaves tasting of nasturtium; everyone gathered it by the handful and ate it eagerly like cattle turned out to grass after a long winter.

The leper set off on his own towards the centre of the island where he could see a grove of umbrella pines. He had the feeling that he knew where he was going even though he had no recollection of ever having been here before. The scent of the sage, the taste of *porcella*, the colour of the birds, the white tenacity of the ashphodel and now the sound of pine cones splitting to release their seeds, it all reverberated like nostalgia for something he had forgotten.

He reached a stone wall built around a little field in which young barley was growing. This surprised him because he knew that no one was supposed to be living on the island. Beyond the field there was what looked like the ruins of a house and when he got closer he saw the dried body of an octopus hanging with stiffened tentacles from a branch fixed between a crack in the wall. There was no other sign of life; no dog to bark a warning or chickens to scatter in a panic of anticipated slaughter. Just the planted barley and the caught octopus.

The leper went inside the house. It was a single room in which the bed was a pile of soft pine branches, the table was a piece of wood balanced on stones and there were fresh ashes in the open fire. Half a loaf of bread was on the table and the leper picked it up and broke a piece off, tasting that it had been made from the ground roots of some plant and not from barley or wheat.

He could sense that someone was watching him. He went searching around the outside of the house and eventually caught sight of a man dodging among the concealment of the trees. He was naked but partly covered by the length of his hair and his beard. Once he had been seen he began to laugh a shrill nervous laugh like the warning cry of some bird.

The leper sat down with his back to the stone wall of the house and he waited. Slowly the laughing man drew closer and closer, until he sat crouched in front of him, shivering and staring and only occasionally breaking out into a spasm of high-pitched laughter. 'I'm the only man in the world left alive!' he announced in a language which the leper could understand easily. 'I'm the only man in the world left alive!' repeating the words and with no others to follow as if he had forgotten everything else that could be said.

It was only then that the leper remembered how he had been to this island before on his previous journey and he had felt so isolated, so cut off from existence that he had considered staying here, occupying the ruins of a house, catching what fish he could from the sea, maybe even cultivating the scrap of a field where wild barley was growing. He realized then that he could have been this same man who sat shivering with loneliness in front of him.

He returned to where his companions were busy making a fire. He said nothing to them about his meeting. He said nothing to them at all, but sat with them in the silence of his own thoughts.

Twenty-six

The leper was lying on his mattress in the fusty darkness of the hold. The blanket rough on his bare skin. The smell of cat's piss in his nostrils. The bilge water slopping backwards and forwards underneath him. The struggle of the wind in the sails. The sense of the ship as some vast warm-blooded animal into whose belly he had been swallowed.

Something rustled close to his ear; a cockroach perhaps. Something else pattered with nervous delicate feet over his legs – that must be a rat, there were a number of rats living in the hold and they were learning not to be afraid since nothing much could hurt them. They chewed at shoe leather even when the shoes were being worn and made nests in piles of old clothes, their pink babies squeaking for food.

The door out onto the deck had been closed because a storm was rising and that meant there wasn't even a glimmer of light. The old man who lay on one side of the leper started coughing and groaning and then he was pissing into a tin pot and sighing to himself as he did so, as if his life was escaping with this release of liquid.

A cockerel started to crow, disregarding the fact that it was the middle of a starless night. A heavy object rolled across an uneven surface and came to a juddering halt just above the leper's head. He wondered what that was. Once again he remembered the six horses and their hooves grinding down on him.

He ran his hand over the mosquito bites on his calves, over a cut that hadn't healed, over the soft hollow of his own belly, the slipperiness of his scars, the density of his pubic hair. He brought the hand out from under the blanket but he couldn't see it even when he held it in front of his face. Nevertheless he could imagine it: a pale, nervous, questing thing, its five tentacle legs always trembling even when he tried to hold them steady. He sent his hand to hunt blindly in the dark. It found the sticky damp of the wooden floorboards, then the smooth cold metal of the locked box of possessions. It went further and reached the edge of the mattress on which Sally was lying, meeting with the warmth of an arm and a shoulder before withdrawing again.

You could tell how everyone crowded into this cluttered space was wide awake in anticipation of the storm's fury. They had seen the clouds thickening along the horizon. They had heard the captain giving the order to furl the sails. The ship's two anchors had been lowered in the hope that the great hooks might catch hold of something on the sea bed that would stop them from being swept along helplessly by the wind, but the water was too deep and the anchors had found nothing.

Now the wind was coming from all four directions at once, making the ship thrash from side to side, and while it was being held in this trap the storm broke directly above it. The singing cries of the sailors were drowned by the roar of thunder and the crack of lightning. The ship groaned as the tarred seams of her sides were split and salty water began to seep down the inside walls, spreading over the floor and soaking into blankets and mattresses, into bread and biscuits, old clothes and saints' bones.

One wave hammered urgently at the closed door of the hold while the next broke through the splintered wood and raced down the stairs, rushing among the men and women who lay there helpless in the darkness.

Chests and boxes were smashed, bursting open and vomiting out their contents. Bottles broke and collided with piss pots and basins. Some of the pilgrims were able to cling to the central pillars for safety, the rest were swept like rubbish into loose heaps.

The leper was lying in a corner, barricaded by mattresses that were not his own, soaking wet and dizzy from something which had hit him on the head. People were crying and praying and screaming in a great soup of noise all around him, but he felt very relaxed and almost contented. He was not afraid. He thought that the ship was bound to sink and he was bound to die and he welcomed the idea of ceasing to be. It was, after all, something he had longed for ever since his first escape from Venice and now at last it was coming upon him and this was the end.

He stared into the darkness and it was as if his eyes were emitting beams of light so that he could see whatever they gazed on. He saw the hold filled with dark water like some underground cavern and bodies lying on mattresses all around him as if on little rafts. He knew every one of them because they were all the people he had ever known in his life; friends, lovers and chance acquaintances all floating and tilting around him. Coming to say goodbye perhaps, or just to witness his departure. On one mattress he saw the elephant's skull which he had searched for as proof of his own veracity, and on another there was an angel looking like a huge dragonfly, its wings bedraggled from the water. And Christ with bare feet, and a man with a wide mouth and leaves growing out of his face, and even a mermaid, her smile made lascivious by her sharp teeth. All companions of one sort or another.

The storm continued unabated for how long? Two nights at least, perhaps three. It was difficult to keep any track of time.

And then something happened. The leper was drifting in the circles of his own thoughts when he noticed the change. 'Listen!' he said to himself and to anyone else who could hear. 'Listen!' And although the waves and the wind were still thundering and the ship was still groaning from the struggle, there was a silence like bated breath somewhere at the centre of all the chaos.

Within that silence the leper became aware of the sound of hands clapping in a fast rhythm of celebration and then voices chanting 'Holy, Holy, Holy,' softly at first but with a gathering intensity.

He shuffled forward on hands and knees over the heaped bodies, the sodden mattresses, the broken boxes and through the swamp of dirty water. He clambered right over someone's face and hardly heard the muffled cry of protest. He aimed for the broken door. He climbed up the five steps and out on the deck. A group of exhausted sailors were gathered together, clapping their hands and chanting while watching a ball of fire that was balanced in the ship's rigging.

It was not a threatening fire. It quivered and shook with something like tenderness or benevolence. The leper saw how it crept with a tentative bouncing movement along the stretched line of a rope, pausing every so often to gaze at the men who stood and stared at it. They were still chanting 'Holy, Holy, Holy,' but more softly now as if they were afraid of disturbing the blessing they could feel dropping down on them like rain.

It was Saint Elmo's Fire, everyone knew that. The saint had seen them being battered by the storm and he had taken pity on them. He had sent his fire as a sign that they would come to no harm. They would all live.

The pilgrims began to creep cautiously up onto the deck to witness this miracle of light. It stayed there waiting for them, moving with delicate curiosity from one part of the ship to another until everyone had been sure of seeing it. Then it was gone.

The storm was not quite over but it had lost its fierceness and anyway no one was afraid because they knew that they were safe with the saint watching over them. The sailors set to work, singing to each other with renewed courage in their voices. The pilgrims sang as well while they tried to put some order into the confusion of their sleeping quarters.

Within a few hours the sea had become quiet and placid and a soft wind was blowing them towards a new island and the port of Modon. The leper felt very quiet too. It was as if he had died and had been brought back to life again.

Twenty-seven

They left Modon after a few days and were on their way towards the island of Candia when a calm descended. It was like that moment in the fairy story when all life stops and nothing moves except for the thorny bushes which go on growing, thickening around the castle and putting an end to any possibility of escape.

The calm descended and they were trapped within it. The air tasted stale and unreplenished; you felt you might suffocate just from breathing it. The birds and the fish had gone. The sun shone within a sickly yellow haze and a mist hung over the motionless surface of the sea, obscuring the horizon and turning the whole world into this one small place.

The oarsmen tried to pull them through but it was as if the sea was holding them back and taking away their strength. After three days what was left of the fresh water in the barrels had turned into a thick and putrid sludge. The wine was sour and too strong to drink. The meat was crawling with maggots that all hatched on the same night. The biscuits were being devoured by weevils, the fruit and vegetables were rotten.

Dark blankets of fleas had moved into the sleeping quarters while the deck was dancing with biting flies and clouds of gnats. Even if you spent two hours combing the lice from someone's hair, they had returned as a somnambulant army before the day was done. There was a disgusting white worm which crawled over you while you tried to sleep, its body filled with blood. The sailors said they had never seen such a worm before and it had no name.

Rats and mice gnawed at blankets and shoes. They walked over faces and licked the moisture from the corner of closed eyes. They had lost the last remnants of their fear and no longer scattered when they were disturbed, but stood there trembling and defiant and seeming to beg for charity.

The captain gave the order that no water was to be given to the animals which were tethered in pens close to the kitchen. During the heat of the day they were silent in their suffering but they cried through-out the night and with the dawn they could be seen licking at the wooden planks to catch the thin covering of dew. All of the poultry, two pigs and a calf died, but since no one had the energy to gut them and cook them quickly enough their rotting carcasses had to be thrown overboard. Not a single shark appeared when the blood spread its message across the water.

One man developed a fever and began to scream in his bed and several others caught the contagion from him. The shoemaker's wife tried to comfort them, but they hardly noticed her presence. Three of them died where they lay.

The leper sat with his companions. Although they had all chosen freely to go on this journey with him, he now felt terribly responsible for them. He felt he should know how to comfort them and to explain how best to endure the heat and the thirst and the agony of waiting for things to change, but he had no energy and no words.

He looked from one to the next. Sally's face was very swollen. She kept licking her parched lips and staring at the haze which covered and obscured the sea. 'The horizon has gone,' she said, and she began to cry but without the relief of tears falling.

The priest was bent over the book of travels. 'We have reached this page and now we must go further,' he said, pointing with his finger at the scrawl of words on a line and then turning the pages on and on as if that was the magic that would undo the spell of their predicament.

The shoemaker's wife confronted her suffering by withdrawing herself from it. She hardly moved her body at all, only the pupils of her eyes expanding and contracting like a cat's. She had bought a silken yashmak from some gipsies on the last island and she wore it all the time, making it impossible to see the emotion on her face. Sometimes she would talk to her husband, discussing things with him and listening to what he had to say.

'What is he telling you?' the leper asked her.

'He is preparing to let go of me,' she replied. 'He says that soon he won't be able to visit me, not even in my dreams. He says he can see the path my life will take and that is enough. I will be cared for.'

The calm was going to lift in a while but there was no way of knowing that with the air still so heavy and unchanged. Sally was gazing into the mist when suddenly she scrambled to her feet, shouting and pointing, 'My husband! I can see him, there in his boat! He is waiting for me! I am going to him!' And before anyone had time to fully understand what was happening she leapt over the side of the ship. There was the sound of her body hitting the water's surface and then silence.

The others were too stunned to speak. They stared at each other in disbelief, each hoping that what they had seen was nothing more than a private fantasy engendered by the claustrophobia of the day. And then as the reality of what had happened grew stronger they peered over the side of the ship, looking for a sign of life or death, but there was nothing there. They searched the mist for the boat which Sally had seen, but if it had been there before it was gone now and so they gave up and sat huddled together, blank and desolate.

The leper was remembering everything he knew of Sally. He saw her as she first appeared to him when he walked into the village: her haunted moon face and how she had taken the book of travels and wrapped it close to her breast. He saw her again poised by the seashore in the bitter cold when he had pulled her back to safety. Only now that she was gone did he understand how close he had felt to her and how much he would miss her.

The priest and the shoemaker's wife were also turning the thought of Sally over and over in their minds. She hovered close to them like a ghost, appearing and disappearing before their eyes, tantalizing them with her presence and her absence. And all the time the calm was shifting and dispersing so that when they looked up it was gone and they could see the steep mountains of the island of Candia, silhouetted against a clear sky. Fish were in the sea. Birds were wheeling and calling overhead.

The town they entered was very beautiful, with watercourses and windmills and fine houses. An ostrich in a walled garden was stalking among the wilting flowers on big feet.

At this time of year hundreds of falcons flew over the island and the people caught them in nets and sold them in the market. The leper bought one: tethered and hooded, fretful within its sudden captivity, uttering little screams of rage and despair.

He went with it on his arm to the high plain of Lessithi. The people who lived here had been driven out long ago; their houses destroyed, their fields laid waste, their fruit trees cut to the ground. Herds of wild ibex moved among the ruins. It was here that the leper released the falcon. He watched it fly in widening circles until it was out of sight.

Twenty-eight

The journey continued. They spent several days on the island of Rhodes, but avoided Cyprus because it had been raided by pirates: houses burning in the town of Paphos, dogs howling and no people anywhere.

They followed the coast of Turkey and were close enough to the land to see men riding on donkeys and the tombs of the dead cut into the white cliffs of rock like giant doorways into another world. But they stopped only briefly to replenish their water supply. The wind was behind them, they had enough food and they were afraid of being attacked by the Turks.

A mood of elation was growing among the pilgrims with the Holy Land now so close. People sang and danced. One man climbed up into the ship's rigging and said he would not come down until they had arrived.

One morning they were woken by the blowing of

trumpets much earlier than usual and when they stumbled out onto the deck the sailors pointed at a range of mountains which looked like a bank of pale clouds. And that was their destination.

They sang the Te Deum. They cried and kissed each other and some even fainted with emotion. A man who had been drunk since they left Venice was suddenly sober and a man with a fever was carried up from the sleeping quarters and left to blink in the bright sunshine, a wild delirious smile on his face.

They dropped anchor in the shallow waters of the Bay of Jaffa and a school of dolphin came to leap around the ship. Everyone felt this was a good sign. But they could not go ashore until permission had been granted by the Governor of the region, so they had to wait for him to arrive, gazing longingly at the land from the sea.

The leper remembered how the city of Jaffa had been bustling and prosperous the last time he saw it. It was now in ruins and nothing was left except for a line of broken towers and walls among the rocks and the encroaching sand. He wondered who had attacked it and why, but there was no way of finding out.

He knew that Jonah had been vomited from the belly of the whale onto this beach and the giantess Andromeda had been chained to these rocks while she waited for the dragon to come for her. He could just see a few rusty links of the chain fixed to the rocks that were still stained with the dragon's blood, and several huge rib bones were sticking up out of the sand like the wrecked hulk of a ship. And there were the dark mouths of the caves where Saint Peter had lived while he was preaching here and where the pilgrims would be expected to stay.

The ship remained at anchor in the shallow nervous sea. More and more people were congregating within the ruins of the city. They came drifting in from the parched landscape on donkeys and camels and on foot. They set up their mushroom tents among the broken walls and tethered their animals to the stumps of pillars. The smoke from their fires dissolved into the blueness of the sky and the smell of spices and roasting meat was carried on the air. The pilgrims stood in anxious groups on the deck and watched the Saracens; they were so close you could count the rings on their fingers.

Finally after nine days of waiting there was a change. The people on the land began to wave and beckon excitedly. The Governor and the Prior from the Monastery of Saint George had arrived. A table had been set up on the beach and the pilgrims could go ashore.

As soon as they landed the Saracens surged around them, snatching at the hem of a cloak, reaching out to touch hair or skin, grasping at sacks and staffs and bodies. A man tugged at the leper's sleeve with a look of desperate entreaty on his face. A young boy thumped the shoemaker's wife on the back with the palms of both his hands, but when she turned to shout at him he offered her the gentlest of smiles, as if the attack had been intended as nothing more than a form of greeting.

The pilgrims were herded together to stand like sheep in front of the Governor, the Prior and a scribe who was seated between them. The Prior nodded his head wearily and made the sign of the cross over each man or woman who was presented to him. The scribe was fluent in many languages. 'What is your name and your country?' he asked, first in Italian and then trying German, French, English and Dutch, spitting the words out like the accusation of a crime. The Governor hardly bothered to look up, but signed the documents that were set before him with an expression of utter despair on his face.

And then they were driven stumbling forward into the caves of Saint Peter where the stink of stagnant water, human excrement and rotting meat was so overwhelming that some of the pilgrims tried to escape back into the fresh air. But their way was blocked by men with swords.

After a little while flaming torches were brought in

to illuminate the rough walls, the high ceiling, the pools of dirty water and the carcasses of two sheep. But before the pilgrims had lost all hope a crowd of noisy strangers burst in bearing a whole market of goods for sale. There was brushwood to lie on, and rushes to cover the filth on the floor. The scent of aromatic gums and sweet spices filled the stagnant air. One man had a roll of white muslin cloth which he sold in lengths so that it could be hung in drifting folds around a bed. Another had a box of sparkling jewels. Two women carried trays of bread and cakes, fried eggs and fresh dates. A donkey bore the weight of a metal urn filled with a warm honey drink.

At night a man with a club stationed himself at the entrance to the cave and anyone wanting to go outside had to be polite to him and pay him a fee. But during the day the pilgrims could go wherever they wished.

So there they were, helpless and passive, unable to continue on their way until some new order was given. The leper passed the time by going walking on his own along the shore. He examined the dragon's bones. He picked up the black oyster shells that were scattered everywhere on the sand, their thick-lipped bodies buckled and twisted with age and the battering of the waves. He found a freshwater spring that bubbled into a pool only a few yards from the reach of the sea, but it was only when he put his hand into the water that was so icy-cold it made his bones ache, that he suddenly found himself remembering how the first signs of his sickness had crept up on him, all those years ago.

Then, just as now, he had been staying with the other pilgrims in the caves. From the moment of arriving at Jaffa he had been strangely elated, with a sense of having escaped from the net of his own sadness, a new life lying ahead of him and the door of the past banged firmly shut. But then one night he had become aware of a sensation like fear itself rushing with the blood in his veins and beating with the pumping of his heart, and in the morning he saw that red swellings were appearing on his body, starting with the left side of his neck and spreading down across the shoulder and up into his jaw, making his tongue bloated and slurring any attempt at speech. He felt then as if he was metamorphosing into some other creature, his skin so tight and hot it must burst open to reveal whatever monster lay beneath its surface.

For three days the swellings and the fear that went with them moved over his body, but then at last they began to subside and he presumed the danger was over. He went walking along the coast. He stopped to look at the dragon's bones and picked up the black oyster shells. He reached the spring and put his hand into its icy cold water. And that was when he saw that his hands were covered in scaly patches, the skin breaking off into silvery fragments like fish scales. Even as he watched he could see this transformation taking place and could feel the sickness tightening and shrinking over the entire surface of his body. His scalp became bumpy and rough to the touch. An exhausting, aching pain was devouring his flesh and hammering at his bones.

'The sadness that I carried inside me is eating through my skin and it has turned me into a leper,' he thought to himself. 'It has cut me off from the world and the people who inhabit it.'

Under the protection of the night he returned to the caves and hid himself, cowering like an animal in a dark corner. And when it was time for everyone to leave and make their way towards Jerusalem he did not join them. He stayed in hiding and might have died of thirst and starvation, had not a man called Caiphos found him there and brought him into the glare of the daylight.

Caiphos examined the leper's blistered, damaged skin and shrugged his shoulders as if to say, 'It will pass.' He gave him food and water and a different cloak with a big hood that enveloped him completely and concealed his face. He helped him to make a clapper from the wooden boards that bound his book of travels and then showed him the road that he must take.

He sat there remembering this huge sweep of time with his hand still immersed in the pool of biting cold water. And when finally he removed his hand it was so numb that it hardly seemed to belong to him and he could not command the fingers to move. But it was smooth and clean and uncontaminated by the marks of sickness.

Twenty-nine

They were in the caves for about a week before a man came and told them that everything was ready and they could leave. He led them to a place among the rocks where donkeys and their drivers were assembled and waiting.

They set off in a slow cavalcade, travelling through rolling hills in a south-easterly direction. The land was like a carcass stripped of its skin to reveal the sharp bones and desiccated flesh. There was nowhere to hide; no protection from the cruelty of the sun by day, the cold emptiness of the moon and the stars by night. The howling of hyenas, the braying of the donkeys, shiny black scorpions that hid under stones and were quick to attack although their sting was not dangerous. A small-bodied hare racing towards them like an arrow and passing close enough to brush against the donkeys' legs, but no sign of the enemy it was escaping from.

Sometimes they came across evidence of a patch of land having been cultivated quite recently and then deserted for no apparent reason. Walls enclosed barren fields. Broken wells gave shelter to a few snakes. Exhausted fruit trees leant against each other, their branches withered from neglect.

They entered the town of Gath where the giant Goliath had been born, but nothing remained of it except for the foundations on which houses had stood and fragments of pottery and broken glass mixed up with the dust on the road.

However in the next town of Ram, which was also called Ramleh, they were inundated with human activity. Wave upon wave of noisy strangers surged around them and somehow managed to be both hostile and welcoming at the same time. The men shouted what sounded like threats from doorways and windows and jostled against the pilgrims with such a violent intimacy that they were often in danger of being toppled from their donkeys. Children threw stones and then stared with blank defiant faces as if that proved their innocence. Women hid everything but their darting eyes. But within this delicate balance of emotions everyone was quick to smile, to offer goods for sale or the gift of food and drink, to try to understand what the pilgrims wanted and to lead them this way and that.

The leper and the priest remained quiet and preoccupied in spite of the uproar and they hardly noticed their surroundings, but for the shoemaker's wife it was very different. She was overwhelmed by a sense of familiarity, a sense of coming home after a long absence. She felt she already knew these streets and the life they contained and she searched among the sea of faces for the ones she would recognize and who would acknowledge her. She laughed when the children raised their hands to throw stones and, confronted with the authority of her laughter, they let their stones drop to the ground. She greeted the furtive glances of the women and she was not afraid of the violence of the men.

She was impatient to explore the town. She would have gone alone, but the leper and the priest went with her as she led them through a maze of streets. They entered a covered market where she bought herself a poppyseed cake and a bowl of sticky rice pudding cooked in milk and sweetened with honey. She was shocked when she could not remember the name of this dish. 'It will come back to me,' she said to herself.

The leper stopped to examine some wooden casket boxes. 'What is this?' he asked the man who was selling them, using a phrase taken from the book of travels. 'It is the earth from which Adam was made,' said the shoemaker's wife, as she carefully opened the lid of one of the caskets to show him a powdery red soil as fine as wood ash.

A woman dressed in a robe of faded green silk, with blue-green tattoos covering her chin like crawling insects, was squatting beside a wall and holding a single bunch of mint for sale. Her arm was stretched out as patiently as the branch of a tree, the froth of green leaves at its tip. Her body seemed rooted and still as if it could never be made to move.

The shoemaker's wife bought the mint, her hand settling for a moment in the woman's as she gave her the money. She would have walked away, but just then the strap of her shoe snapped and she bent down to take it off and examine it.

The woman in green made a clicking sound with her tongue. She rose ponderously to her feet and beckoned to the shoemaker's wife to come with her, the priest and the leper following obediently behind. She led them to a tiny shop. She gestured that the two men must wait outside, then ushered the shoemaker's wife in.

The shop was like a tent, the walls and the ceiling hung with folds of brightly coloured cloth. A man was sitting at a bench and working on a pair of shoes. He looked up as his visitors entered and the shoemaker's wife knew him at once. He was quite small with grey eyes and grey hair and the skin of his face was stretched so tight over the bones of his skull that you didn't at first see the tracery of lines showing his age.

He finished some detail on the shoes and when they were ready he gave them to the shoemaker's wife. They fitted her perfectly. She offered him money, but he shook his head and came to stand directly in front of her, their breath intermingling, their bodies almost touching. He took her hand in his and led her through a doorway in the back of his shop. And that was it. She went to another life with him. She was happy to be gone.

The leper and the priest waited patiently outside. After a while the woman in green appeared, but she pushed past them without any sign that she had seen them before. They entered the shop but it was dark and empty. They went searching distractedly through the streets of the town, looking behind bales of silk, sacks of spices and big earthenware pots, as if the shoemaker's wife might be hiding there, waiting for them to find her. They called out her name, their voices small and plaintive among so many other sounds. The priest practised the words he had learnt from the book of travels. 'I want a woman,' he said to whoever would listen. 'I have lost a woman.' People shrugged their shoulders in perplexity and a little boy led them to the open door of a brothel.

They returned to the place where they were staying. Only two of them left now, the other two gone. The leper had a sense of the finality of destiny, as if the loss of Sally and the shoemaker's wife had been inevitable from the beginning of the journey, something that was written in a book as it were, and all that the passage of time did was to turn the pages forward.

On the following morning they left the town of Ram and set off towards the Holy City. The rolling hills were transformed into steep mountains and the track became very narrow as it clung to the slopes and cut its way between high escarpments of rock. The hot sky was silent and oppressive and even the sound of the donkeys' hooves was muffled.

They were following the dried bed of a river when suddenly there was a clatter of falling stones and with terrible cries a group of Bedouin raced upon them. They were riding bareback on moth-eaten camels and they were almost naked, their skin burnt black by the sun, their heads swathed in a swirl of indigo cloth and leather shields slung around their necks to protect the heart and the chest. They carried raised spears and seemed determined to slaughter every one of the pilgrims.

The odd thing was that the donkeys remained quite unperturbed. They continued to plod steadily forward with their heads bowed and hardly seemed to be aware of the lurching bodies of the camels and the screaming of their riders. The pilgrims did their best to imitate the donkeys. One man had his hat pulled off, another lost his staff and a third was knocked from his saddle so that he tumbled to the ground and lay there with his pale legs thrashing helplessly. But nothing else happened and the Bedouin disappeared as fast as they had arrived, taking the hat and the staff with them. The pilgrims saw their camp a bit further along the track: the big skin tents clinging like limpets among the rocks, children playing in the dust, a woman carrying an earthenware jug on her head and the two trophies of war hanging incongruously from the branches of a thin tree.

They spent the next night sleeping on the ground under the blanket of stars and the vastness of the moon. It was very cold. On the next day they were rewarded with the sight of the high walls of Jerusalem crowning a hill and they sang songs as they approached.

At Fish Gate each pilgrim presented the certificate which had been signed by the Governor of Jaffa and, having paid a sum of money, they were allowed to enter the Holy City.

When the leper reached the gate he almost expected to be told that he could go no further. He had been this far before but a man had pulled back the covering of his hood and had seen the encrustation of sickness on his face and he was turned away to wander in whatever direction he chose to take.

But now it was different: no one was stopping him or telling him to go back. He looked about him and everything was new and untrammelled by the burden of the past. He saw the walls of high buildings decorated with geometric patterns of red, black and white brick and the buildings reminded him of nothing he had ever seen before. He heard music playing and caught sight of a woman dancing on a flat roof, her body swaying like a reed in the wind, but she was a stranger to him and brought back no memories.

He asked the priest to lead his donkey to the Hospice of Saint John where they would be staying while they were here. 'I need to be on my own for a while,' he said and his voice no longer seemed to echo through the cavity of his skull with the same lonely resonance he had grown accustomed to.

He set off towards the eastern quarter of the city, with no idea of where he was going or what he might find. He went down steep steps until he reached a narrow and deserted street that was filled with the carcasses of dead animals: camels and horses, donkeys and dogs; some of them swollen and tight with putrescence, others dry and empty. People brought them here because it was so difficult to bury them in the hard, shallow soil outside the city walls, but the leper did not know that. All he knew was what he saw. He stared around him for a while and then he turned and went back the way he had come. He was neither happy nor sad but for the first time in a long while he was empty of recollection. He had entered a place where there were no memories waiting to spring out at him and catch him by the throat and that in itself was an unfamiliar freedom.

Thirty

Here in the city of Jerusalem the leper and the priest were standing in a courtyard outside the Church of the Holy Sepulchre. It was smaller and less imposing than the leper had expected it to be, but then really he had not known what to expect. The glittering dome of a mosque was so close that the two buildings seemed to belong together and now the *muezzin* was calling the faithful to prayer from a high minaret which cast its shadow across the flagstones at his feet.

All the windows had been bricked up and all the bells had been removed from the bell tower, making it seem as if the church had been silenced and blinded. The heavy door was closed and bolted and four Saracen guards with long beards and long sad faces sat cross-legged on a bench by the wall, their swords in their laps.

The carved lintel above the door showed Christ

riding on a donkey on one side and Lazarus being raised from the dead on the other. The people who were gathered around Lazarus were holding their noses because of the stench of his putrefaction. He was looking very frightened by what had just happened to him, and his mouth was wide open. The leper could imagine the shock of being called from a cold tomb like that. He remembered crouching under a black cloth in the church in the village, the priest's voice pronouncing him dead to the world and the sense of relief he had felt from this stepping out of his own body.

He went up to the church door. There was a metal grille set into it and he pressed his face against the bars and inhaled the smell of incense and darkness that lay beyond it. He could see the flickering of a few candles and a shaft of pale daylight which fell down from the ceiling and appeared as solid and luminous as a block of ice.

One of the guards shouted at him and grabbed his shoulder to push him away from the door. It was only then that he became aware of how many people were crammed into the courtyard with more and more of them still arriving. There were the usual foodsellers, merchants and curious onlookers, but there were many hundreds of pilgrims and as their numbers steadily increased you could feel their impatient energy growing stronger and more desperate. They were like a single body, sighing and swaying and longing to break through the closed door of the church.

Just then a woman screamed and fell to the ground, her limbs convulsing and froth on her lips, and this was the signal that released them all. A ripple of noise like a sudden exhalation of breath went through the crowd. Many collapsed in a heap as if they had been cut down like grass. One man stood with his arms stretched out in the shape of the cross and his whole body racked and trembling. Another began to dribble and drool like an idiot. Some were rooted in a trance, others thrashed in a wild agony. The sun moved through the sky, the day became unbearably hot and the guards watched the pilgrims with a sleepy disinterested gaze.

Finally when the evening was drawing in and bats were squeaking and swooping through the air, one of the Saracens took a key from a chain around his waist and went to unlock the door. The crowd surged forward, but the other guards were quick to block the entrance, their hands on the hilt of their swords. The pilgrims had to form a queue, to show their certificate of identity and to pay a fee. Only then were they permitted to step over the threshold.

As soon as they were inside they scattered in all

directions like chickens, stumbling on the uneven floor and shouting to each other across the echoing spaces.

A few of the merchants and foodsellers followed and settled themselves comfortably close to the entrance. Then, with a crash that shook the entire building, the door was slammed shut and locked and bolted, closing the church in upon itself and holding the occupants as prisoners.

How the leper longed for quiet. As well as the urgent babble of human sounds he was now sur-rounded by the whirring of rattles, the ringing of handbells, the shaking of tambourines, something screeching and something else hammering with metal on stone.

He was given a lighted candle to hold and then he was swept along shoulder to shoulder with all the others, moving in a daze from one sacred site to the next. He saw where Christ's naked foot had stepped on a slab of marble, leaving a print that was streaked with blood. Here a dead man had been brought to life, and here the crown of thorns had been put on. And here, and here; every bit of space thick with the knowledge of the things it had witnessed long ago.

He walked up the eighteen steps to the summit of Mount Calvary, pausing to look at Adam's skull trapped within a narrow crack of the rock. He put his hand into the socket inlaid with lead which had held the wood of the cross. The coldness and slipperiness of it shocked him; it was like touching an open wound.

A man was kneeling on the floor with the heavy wings of his cloak spread out around him. He was murmuring a prayer but at the same time the leper could hear a gentle tapping and chiselling noise emanating from the secrecy of the cloak, as he carved his initials or perhaps even the intricacy of a family crest into the white side of the rock. It was such an odd thought to want to leave a memory behind rather than take it with you, to presume that this place which had seen so much would now never forget a man with a hammer and a chisel.

The leper was suddenly tired of people and the isolation of their closeness. He wandered off on his own and went down some steps which led into a vault under the body of the church. The light from a single lantern showed him pillars dripping with moisture, pools of water on the floor and a big conch shell that was fixed into one of the walls, its curling pink mouth inviting strangers to listen to what it had to say.

He put his ear to the shell. At first all he could hear was the suck and hiss of waves beating against the shore, but this changed and became the crackling of the flames of Hell and the voices of the damned crying and begging for mercy. And changed again so that he could hear laughter as well as terror, joy as well as despair. It was as if he was listening to the story of a life, his own or someone else's. The shell even whispered patches of silence to him that carried him drifting through layers of wordless images.

He turned and went back up the steps. He searched for the priest and found him camped in a corner, busy eating hard-boiled eggs and bread by the light of a candle. 'I was thinking of the meal we had on the day we left the village,' the priest said and with that they both shared the same recollection of cold rain, the cry of marsh birds and a long journey only just begun.

When the priest had finished eating he rummaged in his sack and took out the book of travels, a sheet of vellum, a horn of ink and a quill pen. He leant the vellum against the book and he began to write. He wrote down the name of Catherine the Dead Woman, the red-haired girl, the woman who saw devils, the old fisherman, the man who remembered the Great Pestilence and the many others whose lives he had known and shared. And since Sally and the shoe-maker's wife had now gone, he wrote down their names as well.

As soon as the list was completed he took it to the Holy Sepulchre which stood like a marble tent at the centre of the church. The entrance was so low he had to crouch down to avoid hitting his head. A row of lamps illuminated the enclosed space and made the walls tremble as if they were alive. The stone on which the body of Christ had once lain was covered by another slab of stone which had three holes cut into it, each big enough to insert the flat of a hand. The priest pushed the sheet of vellum through one of the holes and held it there. As he did so all the people from the village whose names he had written down stirred themselves and swam before his eyes like a vision of the dead on Judgement Day.

He returned to the leper and without saying anything he lay down on the floor and fell into a deep sleep. The leper sat beside him for the remainder of the night. He watched as the dawn came falling down through the hole in the dome of the ceiling.

Soon afterwards the door of the church was thrown open with a crash of wood reverberating on stone. The four Saracen guards rushed in and with shouts and threats they herded the pilgrims from every corner of the building and back into the courtyard outside.

Thirty-one

The ship was due to return to Venice very soon. Some of the pilgrims had begun to make their way to the Bay of Jaffa and the rest knew they must hurry or they would be left behind.

The priest was eager to go at once. He longed to be back home with such an intensity that he sometimes found himself remembering this journey as if it had already become a thing of the past. And then he would be shocked with the realization that he was still in a distant city among strangers with a huge expanse of land and sea separating him from the world he was accustomed to.

At every place they visited he made a point of finding a pebble and putting it in his pocket until he had accumulated a rattling handful of little stones. He could imagine spreading out his stones on the table in his room close to the churchyard; each one encapsulating a particular memory just as an acorn can encapsulate an oak tree.

He had bought a number of mementos as well and with the thought of leaving he began to wrap them up and place them carefully in his sack. Two pieces of blue silk thread, measured to the exact length and breadth of the Holy Sepulchre; a square of white linen soaked in the Virgin's tears; three leather bags filled with the red dust from which Adam was made; dried roses from Jericho that opened miraculously when you dropped them in a bowl of water and a bunch of thin finger bones with a signed paper to prove they had belonged to one of the children massacred by King Herod. He had considered buying the complete body of a Holy Innocent, curled up like a sleeping cat and with the skin hard and dry, but he decided against it.

It was only when he was packing his possessions that he realized he still had not been to the River Jordan. This was the main thing that had been asked of him, the reason why he had come here. He had forgotten and now it was perhaps too late.

He told the leper that they must go at once to the river, but the leper explained there was no time for such an expedition. He said he had seen bottles of Jordan water on sale in the market and the priest could get one there. But the priest shook his head sadly because this would not be the same.

He was standing outside the Hospice of Saint John wondering what to do next when a young Saracen approached him. He was riding on a donkey and leading another by its bridle. He had a basket of oranges slung over the saddle. He had a crooked back that hunched him forward and made him appear prematurely old, and long tendril arms that seemed to have no strength in them, but swung loosely at his sides. His face was narrow and solemn but when he spoke a huge smile broke across it, splitting it in half and making you forget everything else about him.

'I am Aziz and I am guiding you,' he said with a simple finality, each word carefully enunciated as if he had just learnt to recite them from a book.

'Where are you guiding me to?' the priest asked him.

'I am guiding you to the River Jordan and there you wash your soul clean,' said Aziz and he raised a single finger with great authority, pausing to look at it as if he had never seen such an odd thing before.

'I must find my friend,' said the priest. 'He will come with us.'

But Aziz was not prepared to wait. He said he had only the two donkeys and they must go immediately. He said they were late already.

The priest felt he had no choice in the matter and so he mounted on the second donkey and followed Aziz.

They went through the intricate streets of the city

until they emerged abruptly into a barren landscape. The track began to sink down and down among the empty hills of the Judean Desert, while the air grew so hot and heavy it was difficult to draw it into the lungs.

They entered a wide river valley where the high reeds closed in around them, their flower tips glinting like polished spearheads. The priest could almost believe that he was back in the marshes near his village with the booming of the bitterns and the cat-like mewing of the harriers, but then Aziz was offering him an orange, holding it close to his face and laughing because he didn't see it even though his eyes were wide open. The donkeys' hooves released a metallic smell from the mud which made him sneeze.

Suddenly the curtain of reeds drew back to reveal the River Jordan; a sluggish, dirty-brown sweep of water that hardly seemed to be flowing at all.

'Here you wash your soul clean!' said Aziz confidently. 'I come for you later. You are careful you do not die!' And without waiting for a reply he turned his donkey round and the reeds quickly swallowed them both from sight.

The priest was on his own within the silence which settled over him. He wondered where Sally was and whether she was safe, and the shoemaker's wife. He hoped the leper would not leave without him. He wanted to call for them all by name, but he was afraid of hearing his own unanswered voice. He peeled the orange which Aziz had given him and ate it very slowly, segment by segment. Then he took off all his clothes.

I can see him standing there by the water's edge, as vivid as a painting on glass, the sunlight from outside the window passing through the colours making them dance like flames. The luminosity of his skin. The tight-feathered curls of hair growing across his chest and belly and down his thighs. The nakedness of his long feet. The look of compassion and sadness on his face as our eyes meet across the infinite space which divides us.

He enters the river. The sticky mud slides between his toes and sucks at his feet and ankles. Dark bubbles rise to the surface and break around him. The water is as warm as his own blood.

He swims out from the bank with lazy strokes. He means to swim to the other side but he is only halfway across when he reaches the fast current which runs through the centre of the river. It grabs at him with strong hands. It spins him round and tries to roll him over on to his back. He fights with it as if he is fighting the coils of a snake, the embrace of a demon.

He feels his energy slipping away and the strange lassitude which enters his body is a pleasure more intense than he has ever experienced before. 'I am dying,' he thinks, and he lets go and drifts on the surface of the water like a leaf.

But the river has lost interest in him now that he is no longer prepared to resist it. The same current that tried to pull him down carries him to the bank and deposits him among the reeds. There is a bitter taste in his mouth. The sun dries the mud on his skin into scaly patterns.

When his breathing has quietened and his strength has returned he gets up and finds his clothes. He takes the empty bottle he has brought with him and dips it into the river until it is filled with the murky liquid that almost took his life.

He searches the dark silted earth for a pebble and finds one that is perfectly round. He moves its roundness in the palm of his hand so that it feels like a living thing and then he drops it into his pocket to join the others. Since there is no sign of Aziz he mounts the donkey that has been waiting patiently for him and trusts it to find the way back to the city.

The dusk thickens as he travels. When he reaches the Hospice the leper is no longer there, nor has he left a message to say where he has gone. The priest and a few remaining pilgrims set off for the Bay of Jaffa on the following morning.

Thirty-two

The leper had waited for the priest but then when there was no sign of him he presumed he must have gone, in the same way that Sally and the shoemaker's wife had gone. All of them gone now, leaving him on his own.

He had no wish to return to Venice. That journey had been made and would not be repeated. Instead he planned to set out towards the Monastery of Saint Catherine in the Sinai Desert. He had once glimpsed something of the immensity of that landscape and the possibility of stillness it offered. The image had always remained with him, clear and undiluted by time.

So he packed his few possessions and set off on a donkey with a camel to carry his provisions of food and water. I caught sight of him just as he was going through the city gate, its twin towers like the pieces in a chess set. I decided to accompany him. I wanted to see what he saw, to taste what he tasted and to follow him in whatever direction he chose. And that was how we came to be travelling together, the leper and I.

When I look back I can see the two of us on a road which stretches for mile after mile. Sometimes this road is clearly defined but often it is obscured or obliterated by wind-blown hills of sand, by falls of rock, or by simple neglect because so few people pass this way.

I see us side by side within the changing landscape. Here we stop to rest by a well and under the shade of a solitary tree; here we meet with naked strangers; here we sleep in a cave; here we are watched by a creature which has the body of a lion but the face of a man. Even when we have travelled for several weeks and are far from the city we have left behind, there is no perspective of distance to diminish us, we appear as close as we ever were.

For the first three days we rode over a barren plain scattered with flat stones. It reminded me of the land which the shoemaker had to cross after he died: everything stripped away and no houses or people, no trees or birds or shade, just the plodding eternity of tiny figures, their shadows growing longer as the sun moved through the sky.

Nothing lived on the plain except the snakes which lay tangled together on the hard ground, a writhing knot of them pulling apart with the sound of our approach and slip-sliding into their burrows as if they had never existed.

One evening the leper caught a snake with a forked stick. He cut its body in half, the head still fierce and the tail flickering with anger. He placed the two pieces one on either side of the road and we walked between them because he said this was an old custom that would bring us luck.

We entered the land which was known as The Great Desert. Gusts of sand were drawn up in thin plumes like the smoke from a hundred camp fires. Hills of sand were swelling around us as if there was yeast fermenting in their soft hot bellies. Sand moving and shifting and flowing like water. Our donkeys struggled to wade through it although for the camel it was easy.

We reached a Bedouin encampment. At first I could not understand why these people had set up their leather tents here, with no shelter and no sign of food for their animals. But the leper said there were deep cracks in the rock where you could be sure of obtaining rainwater throughout the year.

Naked children were squatting in the dust. As we drew closer they crowded around us in a noisy circle. 'Pan,' they chanted, 'pan, pan, pan,' holding out their empty hands with this simple request. Swarms of flies were feeding on the cuts in their skin. We gave them dried biscuits which they swallowed whole.

The men showed no sign of aggression towards us. They were also naked apart from a scrap of cloth tied around their hips and indigo blue turbans on their heads. They had no fire but were cooking slices of meat and flat cakes on polished stones which they placed under the fierce glare of the sun. They offered us some of their food with an easy generosity and watched while we ate. The cakes were unsweetened and the meat was leathery, nevertheless it was better than what we had. They gave us water too, which they filtered through a cloth bag. It was thick and white and slightly salty, but not unpleasant to drink.

The women were the last to approach, appearing suddenly out of the dizzy mirage of the land. They wore girdles made of palm leaves with a flap of piebald goatskin to cover their sex. Their long hair was braided and bound on top of their heads and decorated with ornaments of silver and gold, making it appear like shining fruit in the branches of a tree. They were less friendly than the men and the children, stopping before they were close and throwing stones at us while crying out in high ululations which filled me with a strange cold fear.

But now the days and nights of my memory begin to roll into each other as the image of the desert tightens its grip. I see myself riding beside the leper and sometimes he appears to be nothing more than my own shadow. I see myself moving through a blur of shifting colours: blue and green, lilac and purple. The pebbles of a dried river bed are white under my feet while the cliffs on either side of me are as red as blood.

Here is a place where the rock is threaded with a network of gold and here a swirling hollow in the rock which is filled with a dragon's hoard of bright jewels. Here is a boulder that has taken on the appearance of a magnificent palace and next to it is one carved into the form of a human skull, the eyes staring but sightless.

By now we were on the Tih Plateau where the stones were worn as smooth as polished marble from the abrasion of the wind. We had to lead the donkeys forward by their bridles or else they would have slipped and fallen. Even the camel swayed uneasily, its head swinging close to the ground as it groaned with dismay.

For days, or perhaps it was weeks, we had seen nothing growing in this dead land, but then suddenly there was the luxuriance of a patch of thorny bushes and next to them something that resembled an apple tree, but bearing a grey-green fruit which was so bitter even the scent of it made the inside of my mouth feel parched and rough.

We had grown accustomed to the stillness of our surroundings, where nothing moved unless it was blown by the wind, but then we stumbled right into a colony of desert rats; hundreds of them scattering and leaping and bumping against the donkeys' legs before vanishing back into the land's camouflage.

I shall never forget the herd of gazelles, their delicate bodies materializing like mist out of the empty hills. In my surprise I dropped the orange I was holding and one of them darted forward and snatched it up, carrying the golden ball triumphantly in its mouth as if it had caught the sun itself.

We came to an open mine shaft which had been worked for precious metal and next to it an underground hall where anvils and hammers were laid out neatly on wooden benches, waiting patiently for the return of the people who worked here. But they had already been gone for many generations, the leper said, it was just that things were left undisturbed in the desert; time was different here.

And then a cave cut into the yellow side of a cliff. The welcome relief of cool air and partial darkness. The musky smell of an animal that had this place as its home and signs of where its heavy body had pressed into the soft sand on the floor.

The leper and I spent one night together in that cave. His mouth on my mouth so that I breathed his breath as if it were my own. My hands running over the scars where his damaged skin had been healed by the sunlight and I could feel the light touch of my fingers as if his body was mine. When I looked into his eyes I saw myself reflected there.

That night I slept and woke and slept again until I had grown so accustomed to finding the leper lying close beside me that we seemed to have been together for many years. But when the morning came he would not speak to me. He had a strange wistful look on his face. I asked him what was the matter but he only put his finger to my lips to quieten me.

We left the cave and continued on our way until we were confronted by the silhouette of two mountain peaks outlined like two huge heads against the sky. We followed a long descent down into a ravine with the authority of these mountains watching us.

I remember seeing the footprints of an ostrich and thinking that it looked as though a leaf had been walking along the track. And then a lion with the face of a man was observing us from a far ridge and I wondered if this was the creature whose sleeping body had been imprinted on the floor of the cave.

All I can remember of what happened next was passing through a narrow cleft of rock. That was when

I lost the leper. He must have stepped back in the same moment that I was stepping forward. I turned to look for him but he had gone.

Just ahead of me there was a grove of fruit trees and a haze of green where the ground had been cultivated. When I tried to see beyond this image I could not, because everything at once became blurred and indistinct. I knew then that I had reached the edge of the world that the leper had allowed me to share with him. It was the end of the journey. I was ready to go home.

Epilogue

The priest went back the way he had come, rewinding the thread of where he had been, retracing his steps from south to north, from heat to cold, from olive tree and palm to oak and silver birch.

By the time he arrived at the port of Great Yarmouth he had been gone for more than a year and that meant it was over two years since the day on which the mermaid was found washed up on the sand.

He walked along the raised path through the marshes and past the old barn where he and the others had spent the night together with the sound of rats rustling in the straw. The same dog with pale eyes that had watched them go was there waiting for him among the trees, close to the boundary stone, its tail wagging in nervous expectation.

'Where are the others?' the people from the village asked him when he came to their houses. He tried to explain how he had lost them all one by one and they nodded their heads as if they understood what he meant, although they remained perplexed.

The bottle of Jordan water was put into a silver casket and propped up on a little shelf in the church, close to the bell tower. At a certain time of the day the light through the window on which the feathered angel was painted would shine directly onto the casket. It was found to be very good at protecting those at sea from shipwreck and from drowning.

The priest gave away his other mementos of the journey although he kept the pebbles. He set them out in a line on his desk and he would often place one in the palm of his hand and let the place it contained seep into him. And he still had the book of travels which the leper had given to Sally. He read it to himself over and over again until he knew most of the words by heart.

Sometimes when I sit in the sunshine with my back against the rickety wooden hut, close to the fishing boats and the black stone under which the mermaid's hair is buried, I see the priest standing there beside me and staring out towards the horizon. But I never try to talk to him. Nor do I walk down the main street of the village with the ground beneath my feet rutted by the wheels of carts, or peer into the open doors and windows of those battered houses which once reminded me of the nests of birds. Not any more. That time is over. The place has changed and I am a different person now to the one I was then.